Summer's here, and the ~~~~~~~~~~~~~~mood we've got some sizzling reads for you this month!

So relax and enjoy…a scandalous proposal in *Bought for Revenge, Bedded for Pleasure* by Emma Darcy; a virgin bride in *Virgin: Wedded at the Italian's Convenience* by Diana Hamilton; a billionaire's bargain in *The Billionaire's Blackmailed Bride* by Jacqueline Baird; a sexy Spaniard in *Spanish Billionaire, Innocent Wife* by Kate Walker; and an Italian's marriage ultimatum in *The Salvatore Marriage Deal* by Natalie Rivers. And be sure to read *The Greek Tycoon's Baby Bargain,* the first book in Sharon Kendrick's brilliant new duet, GREEK BILLIONAIRES' BRIDES.

Plus, two new authors bring you their dazzling debuts—Natalie Anderson with *His Mistress by Arrangement,* and Anne Oliver with *Marriage at the Millionaire's Command.* Don't miss out!

We'd love to hear what you think about Presents. E-mail us at Presents@hmb.co.uk or join in the discussions at www.iheartpresents.com and www.sensationalromance.blogspot.com, where you'll also find more information about books and authors!

EXPECTING!

She's sexy, successful... and PREGNANT!

Relax and enjoy our fabulous series about couples whose passion ends in pregnancies... sometimes unexpected!

Share the surprises, emotions, drama and suspense as our parents-to-be come to terms with the prospect of bringing a new baby into the world. All will discover that the business of making babies brings with it the most special love of all....

Delivered only by Harlequin Presents®

Natalie Rivers

THE SALVATORE MARRIAGE DEAL

EXPECTING!

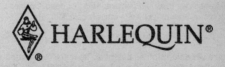

HARLEQUIN®

TORONTO • NEW YORK • LONDON
AMSTERDAM • PARIS • SYDNEY • HAMBURG
STOCKHOLM • ATHENS • TOKYO • MILAN • MADRID
PRAGUE • WARSAW • BUDAPEST • AUCKLAND

ISBN-13: 978-0-373-12735-1
ISBN-10:   0-373-12735-9

THE SALVATORE MARRIAGE DEAL

First North American Publication 2008.

www.eHarlequin.com

Printed in U.S.A.

All about the author...
Natalie Rivers

NATALIE RIVERS grew up in the Sussex
countryside. As a child, she always loved to
lose herself in a good book, or in games that
gave free rein to her imagination. She went
to Sheffield University, where she met her
husband in the first week of term. It was love
at first sight, and they have been together
ever since—moving to London after graduating,
then getting married and having two wonderful
children.

After university Natalie worked in a lab at a
medical-research charity, and later retrained to
be a primary-school teacher. Now she is lucky
enough to be able to combine her two favorite
occupations—being a full-time mum and
writing passionate romances.

For my editor, Sally Williamson

CHAPTER ONE

LILY shivered in the back of the water taxi as it travelled carefully along the foggy Venetian canal. The cold and damp seeped through her suede jacket, chilling her to the bone, but she was grateful for the fresh air. It was warmer inside the polished wooden cabin of the taxi, but it was stuffy, and the movement of the boat made her feel queasy. These days everything made her feel queasy, but at least now she knew why.

She was pregnant.

She closed her eyes and took a deep breath. Pregnant. How was she going to tell Vito?

She'd been living with him for five months, and during that time he'd been the most amazing, attentive lover she could have imagined. But she'd always known that as far as he was concerned it was only a temporary arrangement.

From the start Vito had promised her complete exclusivity and, in return for his fidelity, he'd demanded the same from her. But he'd always made it plain that there was no future for the relationship. There would be no long-term commitment, and categorically *no* children.

But now she was eight weeks pregnant. The stomach bug that she'd thought was taking a long time to clear up was actually morning sickness. And presumably the same stomach bug was responsible for the failure of the Pill.

She shivered again and looked at her watch. Vito would be waiting at the *palazzo* for her, wanting to know what the doctor had said. She glanced up as the taxi passed under a familiar arched bridge. In only a few minutes she'd be home.

Suddenly, despite her apprehension about telling Vito her news, she couldn't wait to be with him. A baby might not have been his plan right now, but she hadn't got pregnant deliberately. Vito would understand. He was a rich and powerful man, used to things going exactly the way he wanted, but he wasn't unreasonable. He might be surprised, shocked even, but after he had time to absorb her news she was sure that everything would be all right.

She'd always wanted a family, and now that she thought about it she couldn't think of anyone she'd rather have as the father of her children. He was a successful and influential businessman, but she'd also seen the loving, tender side of him. He wouldn't reject his own baby just because it was unplanned.

It was eerily quiet as the taxi stopped at the watergate entrance of the *palazzo*. The fog muffled the sounds of the city, and all Lily could hear was the lap of the water against the marble steps. She paid the driver and gratefully accepted his hand as she climbed unsteadily out of the boat. Then she made her way upstairs, where Vito was coming out of his study to greet her.

Her breath caught in her throat, and she hesitated on the top stair, just staring at him—soaking up the absolute masculine perfection of Vito Salvatore, her lover.

Over six-feet tall and broad shouldered, he carried himself with the physical grace and power of an athlete.

His black hair was slightly wavy, and it was brushed back from his strong forehead to reveal his breathtakingly handsome face.

She'd often wondered if she'd ever get over how amazing he was. It didn't matter whether he'd been away on business for a few days or whether they'd just been in different rooms for a few minutes—whenever she laid eyes on him after they'd been apart, her heart fluttered and excitement coiled through her. After knowing him for ten months and living with him for the past five months, she was still overwhelmed by the pure thrill of being with him.

'You have returned at last.' Vito caught her with his blue eyes as he closed the distance between them and swept her into his embrace.

'Hmm.' Lily snuggled against his strong chest, pressing her face against his velvety-soft black cashmere sweater. She breathed deeply, drawing his scent into her lungs. Safe in his arms, she felt so much better. The nausea she'd suffered in the water taxi was already a distant memory.

'I tried to call you,' Vito said, lifting her face gently for a lingering kiss. 'But then I found your phone in the bedroom.'

'Sorry.' Lily looked up into his gorgeous face. As always his kiss had the power to make all thoughts fly out of her mind. 'I forgot to charge it.'

'Are you all right?' Vito asked, catching her hands in his. 'You're so pale and cold. Come and sit down. Would you like a warm drink?'

'I'm fine,' Lily replied, letting Vito lead her into his study. 'A glass of cold water would be lovely.' She smoothed her fingers over her hair, suddenly apprehensive again. Now she knew why she'd gone off tea and coffee—and in a minute she'd have to tell Vito.

'I thought Carlo was taking you to your appointment,' Vito said, looking over his shoulder at her as he dropped ice cubes into a glass and poured mineral water from a frosted bottle. 'I don't like you taking public taxis, especially when you aren't feeling well.'

'I was all right,' Lily reassured him. 'I thought I might want to walk a while—the fresh air makes me feel better.'

'Still, if I'd known you were going to dismiss Carlo I would have accompanied you myself,' Vito said, slipping his arm around her waist and guiding her over to a sofa by the window. 'I don't know how you persuaded me not to cancel my meeting.'

Lily ran her hand over her long blonde hair again as she sat down. The humidity of the fog had made it frizz. It was absurd to worry about what she looked like at a time like this, but somehow the enormity of the situation suddenly made it easier to focus on smaller things.

'What did the doctor say?' Vito asked, looking at Lily with concern. Her heart-shaped face really was incredibly pale, and there were dark smudges of fatigue under her expressive hazel eyes. 'Do you need antibiotics?'

'No,' Lily said.

She was smoothing her hands over her hair. Vito recognised the nervous gesture. Since they'd been together he'd grown used to her body language, but he couldn't imagine why she was anxious now.

'Then what is it?'

Fear that there might be something seriously wrong suddenly sliced through him like the blade of a knife. He dropped to his knee beside her, and took her chilly hands in his. The thought of Lily ill was unbearable. 'What did the doctor say?' he pressed. 'Do you have to go back for tests?'

'No.' Lily hesitated, looking at his expression. His

black brows were drawn down with concern, creating two vertical creases between his eyes. She was close enough to wonder at their amazing colour—the incredible vibrancy of sky-blue that made her feel like summer had come, rather than the cold and damp of early spring that still felt like winter.

But she'd worried him—something she'd never meant to do. She should tell him the truth at once.

'I'm pregnant.'

Lily could not have prepared for what happened next. She'd anticipated surprise, maybe even displeasure. But she'd *never* expected the sudden dramatic change in his expression—as if cold steel-shutters had dropped down over his features. Nor the brutal finality of his words.

'Pack your things.' He jerked abruptly to his feet, letting her hand fall from his fingers as if he could no longer bear to touch her. 'And get out of my house.'

CHAPTER TWO

LILY opened her eyes and looked groggily at the clock. Damn! She was late.

'Aren't you up yet?' Anna said, already smartly dressed for work, walking across the open-plan lounge to the kitchen area of her flat. 'I thought you had that presentation this morning. You know—the big make-or-break one.'

'Yes, it's at nine o'clock.' Lily pushed herself up into a sitting position on the sofa. She was so grateful to her friend for letting her stay since Vito had thrown her out, but this sofa wasn't exactly the most comfortable place she'd ever slept.

'Oh dear, you look awful,' Anna said. 'I thought morning sickness was only supposed to last the first few months.'

'So did I.' Lily moved and breathed slowly in an attempt to keep her stomach calm.

'Here,' Anna said, placing a glass of milk on the coffee table. 'Good luck this morning,' she added, already halfway to the front door.

Lily picked up the milk and took a careful sip. It was cool and comforting, and within a couple of minutes she felt her stomach start to settle enough for her to manage a quick shower and get ready for work. Thank goodness for Anna, who'd remembered one of her colleagues talking about how milk had worked wonders for the nausea she'd suffered from during pregnancy.

Forty-five minutes later Lily climbed out of a black cab she could ill afford, and hesitated on the wide London pavement, staring up at the imposing steel-and-glass building that was the home of L&G Enterprises. It was a subsidiary of the Salvatore empire, and a menacing shiver ran down her spine at the thought that Vito might be inside. But if she'd really thought, even for a moment, that there was any chance of him being anywhere near, she would *never* have agreed to make the presentation today.

She took a deep breath, gripped her heavy briefcase tightly, and walked into the building. A long blonde coil of her curly hair was bouncing in front of her eyes, so she tucked it back forcefully behind her ear. She'd been so late that there hadn't been time to straighten and style her hair properly. She'd settled for pulling it back tightly into a twist at the nape of her neck, but it was already showing signs of breaking free.

It was important she did well this morning. So far she hadn't managed to find the permanent job she desperately needed. But, if luck was on her side today, this could be the break she needed. She'd approached her old boss at the computer-software company she'd been working for when she'd met Vito, and as a personal favour he'd been prepared to offer her a chance. If she could sell his company's web-conferencing system to L&G Enterprises, he'd give her a commission and find her a permanent job.

'But didn't Suzy Smith set up the pitch?' Lily had asked, thinking of the flamboyant brunette who'd willingly stepped into her shoes when she'd handed in her notice so that she could move to Venice to be with Vito.

'She did,' Mike, her old boss, had conceded. 'But honestly, Lily, she won't be able to cut it. L&G are a notoriously hard sell. Trust me, Suzy will be glad to hand this one over to you—she even tried to persuade me to take it on.'

'Why don't you?' Lily had smiled wryly, realising she was halfway to talking herself out of this job opportunity.

'Because you're better,' Mike had said truthfully. He might be a computer genius, and was making a success of his small business, but sales spiel was not his greatest strength. 'You know your stuff,' he'd continued, pulling out all the necessary files and information for the presentation. 'And you won't let those stuck-up executives throw you off your stride.'

And now here she was, walking into a company owned by Vito Salvatore—the man who had thrown her out onto the streets of Venice like a piece of trash because she'd made the mistake of accidentally getting pregnant.

Six long weeks had passed since that awful day in March, but Lily was still in shock over the way he had treated her. Although at the time she'd hardly dared to believe her luck at being with such a wonderful man, she really had thought everything was going well with him. Until she'd discovered in the most appalling way that he *wasn't* really so wonderful—otherwise how could he have tossed her aside right when she'd needed his support?

With a determined effort she pushed memories of Vito and the way he had treated her to the back of her mind. Focussing her thoughts on the task in hand, she walked briskly up to Reception, and gave her name and the name of the company she represented. That was the only way she'd got through the last six weeks—by refusing to think about the brutal way Vito had betrayed her and their unborn child

She had no choice. She had to keep it together because she needed to find a job. Then she could make a home for herself and the baby.

'We've been expecting you.' The receptionist spoke without smiling, and handed Lily a visitor's badge. 'Samuel will escort you up to the meeting room.'

'Thank you.' Lily smiled brightly and pinned the badge onto the jacket of her ivory linen-suit. Then she glanced round to see a sullen-faced young man she presumed was Samuel walking across the lobby towards her.

He gave no sign of wanting to engage in small talk, so she followed him silently to the elevator and up to the executive floor, where he showed her to the room that had been booked for her presentation.

Vito had described L&G Enterprises to her as one of his smaller business interests, but there was nothing small about the glass-walled executive meeting-room that she found herself in. This certainly wasn't going to be a cosy pitch, she thought, looking at a vast smoked-glass table surrounded by black-leather chairs.

She had just finished setting up when she heard a voice behind her.

'Ms Smith, I assume?'

Lily plastered a bright smile on her face and spun round to see a short, balding man dressed in a dark suit. She recognised him from his photograph on the company website—he was the head of Corporate Communications.

'It's Lily Chase, actually,' she said, holding out her hand to him. 'I'm very pleased to meet you, Mr D'Ambrosio.'

'Decided to send in the big guns, did they?' D'Ambrosio asked. He let his beady eyes slide over her in assessment, and held onto her hand for far too long.

'You could say that.' Lily smiled. One of the most important rules in sales was always to appear bursting with confidence, even if it sometimes went against the grain. She retrieved her hand and resisted the urge to rub it vigorously on her straight skirt. 'L&G Enterprises is potentially a very important customer, and it was felt that I have the necessary experience to explain our product fully.'

'Hmm.' D'Ambrosio looked unimpressed. 'Let's get started,' he said, sitting down at the immense glass table as another group of suited people came in. One of them, a woman wearing scarily high heels, was talking on her mobile phone in a loud, insistent voice. Another, a young man in his twenties, sat down, opened his laptop and started scrolling through his emails.

Lily looked at the assembled executives, wondering if she should let the woman finish her phone call before she started. They were an arrogant bunch, and she'd long since learned not to expect much common courtesy from this type of person—if she didn't catch their attention quickly, it wouldn't be long before they were all talking on their mobile phones or looking at their laptops.

'What are you waiting for?' D'Ambrosio barked. 'We haven't got all day.'

Lily straightened her shoulders, smiled brightly, and started her pitch.

Vito Salvatore strode through the building in a thunderous mood. He couldn't get his recent visit to his grandfather out of his mind.

Giovanni Salvatore had always been such a force in

his life—a formidable head of the family, an important role model and, most importantly, a dependable father figure when Vito's parents had died in an accident.

But now he was a sick old man, clinging tenaciously to the last months of his life.

'Make me happy before I die, Vito,' Giovanni had said.

'*Nonno*, you know I would do anything for you.' Vito had sat beside him and had taken his grandfather's frail hand in his own. It shocked him to feel the weakness of his grip, feel the constant tremor in his fingers.

'Let me know my name will continue.'

Vito had squeezed his grandfather's hand in reassurance, but he hadn't been able to speak. He'd known what was being asked of him—but how could he promise something that was never going to happen?

'You're thirty-two years old. It's time to settle down,' Giovanni had urged, fixing him with a surprisingly sharp stare. 'You run through women like there's no tomorrow, but you need to stop and think about the future. My days are numbered. Before I die I want to know my great-grandchild is on the way.'

Vito had stood up and turned to look down out of the high-arched window at the many boats on the Grand Canal below. His grandfather was a stubborn old dog. Even as his health declined he'd refused to leave the baroque *palazzo* in one of the busiest parts of Venice.

It had been his home for more than seventy-five years, and he'd declared the constant noise of tourist and business traffic beneath his windows didn't bother him—what would finish him off would be putting him out to pasture in one of the family's rural estates on the Veneto plain. And in truth Vito liked having him in the city where he could oversee the care he was receiving.

He only hoped that he would be able to live out his

days at home. Certainly his fortune would cover the necessary costs of medical professionals to attend him.

'Everything will be all right, *Nonno*,' he'd said, turning to place an affectionate kiss on the old man's cheek. How could Vito break his heart by telling him that the Salvatore line would stop with him?

He pushed the memory aside and continued to stride along the carpeted corridors of the executive floor, unaware of how his expression was scattering employees in front of him. He wasn't in the mood to deal with the directors of L&G Enterprises, but nevertheless he would attend the board meeting.

Suddenly he stopped in his tracks and stared through the glass wall of the meeting room. He could not believe his eyes.

Lily Chase.

Seeing her standing there felt like a sledgehammer blow to the guts. Her betrayal was still a fresh wound and, as he looked at her, he could almost feel her twisting the knife. His heart started to thud furiously beneath his ribs, and he clenched his fists at his sides.

No one betrayed Vito Salvatore and got away with it—but that was exactly what Lily Chase had managed to do. The night he'd discovered what she had done, he'd been so shocked that he had simply thrown her out. It was *so* much less than she'd deserved.

And now, as if to rub further salt into his wounds, it was obvious that she'd fallen on her feet. Because here she was, bold as brass, coolly making a presentation to his communications team—as if she didn't have a care in the world. And as if she had nothing to fear from him.

He looked her up and down, automatically checking for signs of pregnancy, but there was no evidence of her condition yet. If anything she'd lost weight, making her look incredibly thin. The linen suit she was wearing was unflatteringly loose and baggy, and her hair was tied back in an uncompromisingly severe style.

But, even though she wasn't looking her best, he simply couldn't take his eyes off her. With her light-blonde hair and her pale clothing she stood out like a beacon against the dark-suited executives in their dark and gloomy conference room.

Why had she done it?

The question thrust itself forcefully into his mind.

He gritted his teeth, trying not to let his thoughts continue down that path. *He* was always in control. *He* was the one who called the shots, in his private life as well as in business.

All the women in his life understood how it was. Nothing permanent. No strings attached. But always absolute fidelity on both sides while it lasted. Up until the blow Lily had dealt him, that had never been an issue. He was man enough for any woman. Or so he'd thought.

He stared at her through dangerously narrowed eyes, watching her behind the glass. It only took a moment to figure out she'd gone back to her old job, selling web-conferencing software.

Although she looked pale and tired, she appeared calm and in control of the meeting, but he knew she was punching above her weight with this lot. He didn't like the head of Corporate Communications at L&G, and he knew he'd never invest in a new system, even though it was exactly what was needed to bring the company into the twenty-first century.

Why had Lily been unfaithful to him?

The question hammered persistently in his head.

Things had been good between them, both in and out of the bedroom. The time they'd spent together had been a wonderful counterpoint to the cut and thrust of his business life. And the sex... The sex had been nothing short of incredible.

She'd given him her virginity—something he'd considered a truly special gift. But that just made it all the more shocking that she'd fallen into another man's bed so quickly.

The thought of Lily with another man was unbearable. A vein throbbed in his temple and he surged forward, opening the door into the meeting room with a crash.

Lily looked up in shock.

Suddenly she couldn't breathe.

Her worst nightmare had come true—Vito was here.

'What...?' D'Ambrosio started to bluster at the interruption, but the second he realised it was his Venetian boss he fell silent.

Lily dragged a shallow breath into her lungs and felt her heart jolt back into life after the shock of seeing Vito. It began to beat painfully hard as she stared at him.

She'd missed him so much—but he'd hurt her so badly. Looking at him produced a physical ache in her chest. She longed to dash across the room and lose herself in the warm strength of his embrace—but she knew there was no warmth there any more. He'd made that clear when he'd thrown her away.

Despite the pain of seeing him, her eyes roamed urgently over his body as he stood in the doorway. He looked absolutely magnificent. His hand-tailored suit fit him to perfection, but did nothing to conceal his raw, masculine power. She recalled the athletic strength of his lean body only too well. Remembered exactly how it felt to be held close to his hard-muscled form.

But now she shuddered as she saw how intense his

expression was. His bronzed skin was pulled taut across his high, slashing cheekbones, and a muscle was pulsing on his strong angular jawline.

And his blue eyes were fixed on her, in a way that made her blood run cold. She looked straight back, matching his gaze with her own. An icy shiver skittered down her spine as she recognised the steely anger in his eyes. Apart from her final day in Venice, he had never looked at her like that. It was a nasty reminder of how brutally he had ended things between them.

'Tell me why L&G Enterprises should invest in your product.' Vito spoke suddenly.

Lily gripped her shaking hands together tightly and stared at Vito in surprise. She hadn't expected that. She'd thought he would throw her out, or perhaps call Security to do his dirty work for him. She didn't know what game he was playing, but she had no choice but to play along. She certainly wasn't going to turn tail and run from him.

Suddenly a strong smell of coffee assailed her nostrils and a wave of nausea washed over her. She looked down to see a steaming lake of black coffee spreading across the smoked-glass table from D'Ambrosio towards her laptop computer. Vito's dramatic arrival had obviously startled him into spilling his drink, but he was making no move to clean it up.

He looked at her, and with a shock Lily realised he was expecting her to do it. God, he was arrogant! But now, with Vito standing there staring at her, she had more to worry about than D'Ambrosio's spilt coffee.

She took a deep breath, inadvertently pulling the sickening smell of coffee deep into her lungs, and moved her laptop to one side. Then, looking straight at Vito, she began to speak.

Her voice rang out amazingly clear and steady in the ominous silence of the meeting room as she concentrated on delivering the presentation she had previously prepared.

'…and so this new system will give you the very best in web conferencing, saving your business both time and money, not to mention freeing you from the annoyance of using an outdated system that frequently fails to perform according to basic requirements.'

Lily finished her spiel and continued to match Vito's gaze. She knew it was pointless. Mike had been right—L&G was a hard sell. But now Vito had arrived it was more than hard—it was impossible.

The room was deathly silent as everyone waited for Vito to speak and, out of nowhere, her thoughts suddenly turned to her unborn baby. Vito's child. It still hardly seemed real. Some of the time she almost forgot she was pregnant for a few minutes. But then, even if the nagging nausea wasn't enough to remind her, the constant worry over getting a job so that she could provide for her baby slammed the reality home.

She remembered all the warnings her mother had given her about men, and now she was in exactly the same situation as her mother had once been—ruthlessly cast aside because she'd made the mistake of getting pregnant.

Lily's father had refused to acknowledge her, and had even threatened her mother if she ever revealed their relationship. He had his own 'real' family to protect—a wife and two daughters living in a lovely suburban home.

Lily and her mother hadn't been good enough. They'd been a potential embarrassment, always to remain hidden far away in the countryside where they couldn't do any damage to his impeccable reputation.

Lily knew her father was a first-class hypocrite and, as she'd grown older, she'd told herself she'd been better off without him. But it had been tough growing up without a father. Her mother had found it hard to cope, and that had made life difficult and unsettled for Lily.

'We will take your web-conferencing system on three-months-trial basis.' Vito broke the silence abruptly. 'D'Ambrosio, clean up here. Then take Ms Chase's equipment up to my office.'

'But…' For a second D'Ambrosio looked annoyed by his boss's snap decision, but then he recovered himself and jumped to his feet. 'Of course, it would be a pleasure to do business with you,' he said, holding out his hand to Lily almost desperately. 'Your company's system really does sound very impressive. We'll get it all arranged—my people will meet your people, and…'

In other circumstances, witnessing D'Ambrosio's turnaround from obnoxious to obsequious might have been amusing, but at that moment Vito turned his eyes onto Lily with a penetrating look that made the breath catch in her throat.

'Ms Chase, you will accompany me to my suite.' His voice rolled down her spine like thunder, setting her insides quaking. He'd never spoken to her like that before.

'I…I should make arrangements with Mr D'Ambrosio,' Lily prevaricated. Part of her longed to go with Vito, but the sensible part of her mind told her to keep well away from him.

He was not the man she'd thought she knew—the tender lover who'd taken care of her and made her feel safe. This was a very different man—a heartless beast who'd thrown her out of his house one horrible cold night in March.

That night had turned into an escalating nightmare. The airport had closed early because of the fog, leaving her no escape and nowhere to go.

'Come with me.' His words were nothing short of a command, and Lily found herself moving forward even before Vito's hand closed around her arm.

She gasped as he made contact, and her step faltered. It felt like an electric shock had jolted through her. She turned shakily to look up into his face.

Any hope that still flickered in her heart was extinguished as his hostile gaze knifed through her. The anger that glinted in his blue eyes was so cold and relentless that it felt like shards of ice were piercing her soul.

She wanted to get away, but there was no way out. She wanted to bolt for the door—willingly sacrifice the sale and her potential job—but Vito had her arm.

The glacial touch of his gaze ravaged her like a blizzard, but heat from his hand was steadily burning through the sleeve of her linen jacket, spreading insistently through her chilled veins, making her acutely aware of every single inch of her body.

It only took seconds to reach his private elevator and, before she knew it, he'd pulled her inside with him.

She exhaled with an involuntary whoosh as the doors closed, cutting them off from the rest of the world, enclosing them in a space that suddenly seemed too small to contain Vito. The sheer power of his presence was pressing out in all directions, bouncing off the mirrored walls of the elevator, becoming increasingly magnified with every moment that passed.

It felt like she was trapped inside a capsule with him, in a place that was completely saturated by his powerful presence. The air that flowed around his body, slipping underneath his designer clothes and sliding across his firm bronze skin, was moving sensuously over her too. Every breath she took was laced with his achingly familiar scent, setting her nerves alight, making the tiny space they shared more real and vibrant than the world outside.

His fingers still pressed into her arm, but from the way her heart was racing and her skin tingling it was as if his touch extended way beyond that. It was more like he was running his hands all over her naked body. And in a distant part of her mind she was aware of the elevator travelling up, further away from the outside world. Further away from escape.

Then suddenly the mirrored doors slid open and he stepped forwards, taking her with him. She blinked in surprise as he let go of her arm, momentarily disorientated by her new surroundings, and stared around at the cavernous space she found herself in.

'What is this place?' she asked, saying the first words that came into her mind. The floor was covered in a luxurious light-grey carpet, but there was no furniture apart from one imposing desk which was set to the side near the floor-to-ceiling plate-glass windows.

'The penthouse suite,' Vito responded shortly. 'I have no use for it—it's being converted.'

She glanced around again, slowly regaining a little equilibrium as she put some distance between herself and Vito. She couldn't believe how powerfully her body had responded merely from being confined in a small space with him.

As she looked about, she noticed the marks where furniture had once stood, and shadows on the wall where pictures had been removed. It was a soulless space, like a home that had been gutted.

It didn't seem right that she was in this bleak place with Vito. In her mind her time with him was associated with his *palazzo* in Venice, or even just going out and about with him. It wasn't the level of comfort and luxury that was missing—it was simply being together. Being with Vito had always felt like being home. Now she had no home.

'Where are you living?' Vito asked, snapping her out of her thoughts.

'London,' Lily replied briefly. After the way he'd treated her, she didn't see any reason to let him know how unsettled her situation was.

'Alone?' he probed.

'That's none of your business.' He was standing only a few feet away from her, and she met his hard blue gaze with her own. She didn't want him to think that he intimidated her, even though she was feeling very shaky and uncertain. And she was sure he'd seen how being close to him in the elevator had affected her.

'The baby's father.' He spoke through gritted teeth. 'Are you living with him?'

For the second time that morning, Lily's heart skipped a beat.

Vito's words didn't make sense. He couldn't really mean what she thought he did—could he?

'What are you talking about?' she gasped, laying her hand protectively against her still-flat stomach. 'I know it wasn't planned—but *of course* you are the father.'

He was staring at her from beneath black brows, but the morning light flooding in from the massive windows caught his eyes, making them look almost metallic. For a moment she hardly recognised him. This really couldn't be the man she'd lived with for five wonderful months of her life.

'Don't bother with your lies,' Vito said. 'Just tell me if you are in contact with the father. Does he know you are pregnant?'

'You've made a mistake,' Lily said, still struggling

to process the implications of what he was saying. 'You know I've only ever been with you.'

'I may have been your first lover,' Vito said. 'But I wasn't your only lover.'

'But why do you think that?' Lily gasped. 'I don't understand. Did somebody tell you something about me?'

'Just tell me if the father knows,' Vito grated.

'You *are* the father!' Lily cried. 'There's no one else and there never has been.'

His eyes pinned her for a moment longer, as if he was assessing a cold, emotionless business situation.

'From that, I take it that he doesn't know—or maybe he doesn't want to know,' Vito said. 'Whatever the case, from now on, as far as the world is concerned, the child you are carrying is mine.'

'It is yours.' Lily said hollowly. She felt like she was banging her head against a brick wall.

Still holding her with his cold blue stare, Vito nodded once. The decisive movement of his head was strangely unnerving.

'We will be married immediately,' he announced.

CHAPTER THREE

'MARRIED?' Lily echoed, staring at him in utter shock. She couldn't believe what she'd heard. 'If that's some kind of cruel joke, I'm not falling for it.'

'It's no joke.' Vito sounded completely serious, and was looking at her with the hard expression she was starting to get horribly used to. 'We will be married at once.'

'How can you even ask me that?' Lily gasped. Six weeks ago she would have accepted willingly. A proposal from Vito would have been like a dream come true—but not any more. Now it was more like a nightmare. 'After the way you've treated me, I'd be mad to marry you.'

'I'm not *asking*,' Vito said. 'I'm *telling* you that we will be married. And, as far as the world is concerned, the baby you are carrying is mine. He or she will be brought up as the Salvatore heir.'

Lily's head was spinning and her stomach churning. With every passing second, Vito seemed more and more like a stranger.

Her mother, Ellen, had warned her how men could easily change. She'd had personal experience of it. Lily's father had gone from adoring lover to threatening brute overnight, when Ellen had told him that she was pregnant. That was when Ellen had found out that Reggie had been married all along.

He'd already had a wife and two children, and was steadily working his way up the hierarchy of his father-in-law's accountancy firm. Despite the sweet words of his seduction, he'd never been interested in anything more than a fling with Ellen. Her pregnancy had come as a wake-up call to him. He'd had too much at stake.

If his wife, or her father, had discovered his infidelity Reggie could have lost everything—his family, his professional status and, most importantly to him, the prospect of taking over a successful business when his father-in-law retired.

To protect himself, Reggie had set Ellen up in a tiny country cottage. He'd paid her rent and had made measly maintenance payments for Lily, but it was based on the strict understanding that Ellen could never reveal herself or her illegitimate child to his family.

'Look, I don't know what game you're playing with me.' Lily put her hands on her hips and met Vito's gaze straight on. Her childhood had been blighted by her father's duplicity, and suddenly she felt she'd had enough of dishonesty and secrets to last a lifetime. 'But, whatever you're playing at, I don't have time for it. If you want to buy the web-conferencing system, that's good—I need the commission to get myself a flat. If you don't want it, that's fine too. Just let me leave so I can get on with my life. I have to go find a permanent job.'

She had to get a job so that she could provide for her baby. She couldn't let herself end up like her mother. Or in a situation that was even more financially precarious.

Ellen had been devastated when Reggie had showed his true nature. To find herself blackmailed into silence by the man she'd fallen in love with had been unbearable. But with no one to turn to for help, and a baby to consider, she had reluctantly accepted his financial support. Then, as the years had gone by, she had become increasingly dependent on it.

With her trust in people and her confidence in herself eroded, she'd found it impossible to find a job that fitted around caring for Lily. Eventually she'd found solace working as a volunteer at the local hospice. She'd poured all her energy and love into craft projects to bring enjoyment and satisfaction to the terminally ill patients.

Lily loved her mother dearly, even though her childhood had been extremely difficult. She knew it would break her heart if she found out that Lily was pregnant and alone. Whatever happened, she had to protect Ellen from the truth—at least until she was settled. And the first thing she needed to do was find work, so that her future seemed more secure—financially at least.

'You haven't listened to a word I've said.' Vito looked so cold and unmoving, standing there, that Lily felt a sense of foreboding creep over her. 'You don't need a job, or a flat.'

'I heard you talking, but you haven't said anything that made sense,' she retorted, struggling to shake off the uneasy feeling. She decided to tell him the truth about her current circumstances after all, to try and reason with him. 'I need a job and somewhere to live, because since you threw me out I've been sleeping on my friend's sofa.'

'You need a husband to provide for you and the baby,' Vito said. 'And I am offering far more than just that.'

'We're not living in the dark ages!' Lily gasped. His expression was forbidding, but she ploughed on regardless. 'What are you offering that's so great? Money? Of course it would be great to have a rich husband—but, if I can't have a husband who truly loves and wants his child and me, then I'd rather be on my own.'

'Is that really true?' Vito asked. 'Bringing up an illegitimate child on your own isn't easy.'

'I never said it was.' Lily knew only too well how tough her mother had found it. It had been very hard on her too, living with someone prone to depression and panic, someone who had been only truly happy when she'd lost herself in an art project.

'Think about your child,' Vito pressed. 'How can you consider denying him or her the possibility of growing up the Salvatore heir?'

'You're crazy.' Lily lifted her hand to touch her blonde hair in an exasperated gesture. 'First you accuse me of being unfaithful and deny that this is your baby—then you want to marry me and make the child your heir. What am I supposed to think? It just doesn't seem real.'

She looked up into his blue eyes, and suddenly the way he was looking at her sent a prickle of sensual awareness skittering across her skin. It was as if they were back in the elevator again, trapped in a tiny space that was buzzing with the supercharged electricity that was flowing between them.

'*This* is real.'

He stepped forward, covering the space that separated them in two strides. He still wasn't even touching her—but she knew exactly what he was talking about.

Sexual attraction. A wave of heat was swelling through her body, setting all her nerve endings on fire. Deep down she wanted him to touch her again, wanted to feel his hands moving all over her.

'Maybe it's real,' Lily said, horrified by how husky her voice suddenly sounded as his gaze swept suggestively over her body. 'But it's just hormones—it doesn't mean anything.'

'Your virginity meant something to me,' Vito grated. His eyes looked impossibly dark, and a muscle started pulsing on his jawline. 'Until I found out it was meaningless to you—how quick you were to give your body to someone else.'

Suddenly an expression that was almost savage ripped across his features and he seized her, bringing his mouth down forcefully on hers.

Lily's heart lurched and she reeled in shock as he kissed her, but he had her firmly in his powerful grip. He had never been rough with her before, but her body was responding immediately, hot desire for him building inside her.

Despite the feeble protests her mind was trying to exert, the tension in her muscles yielded until she was pliant in his arms. He pulled her tight against him, so that she could feel the wonderfully familiar heat of his body burning through her linen suit.

Her lips softened and opened beneath his, allowing his tongue to sweep inside.

Oh! How she had missed him—how she had longed to be close to him again. It wasn't just the physical intimacy that she craved, although she was kissing him back with a fervency that was making her head spin. She'd missed the amazing relationship that she'd thought they had together. She'd missed him so badly.

His hands were holding her head now, tilting it backwards as he plundered her mouth in a kiss that delved into the very depths of her spiralling desire for him. He had released his grip on her body, but she continued to press herself against him, revelling in the pure masculine power she could feel radiating from his hard form.

Her arms snaked around his back, slipping inside his jacket. Then, almost of their own volition, her hands started to tug at his shirt. She longed to feel his skin under her fingertips, feel his muscles flex and ripple under her palms.

Suddenly she realised what she was doing.

'Stop!' With a monumental effort of will, she broke away from his kiss and forced herself to take a step back from him. 'This isn't what I want,' she gasped, walking shakily across to the huge plate-glass window that overlooked the City of London.

'What do you want?' he asked abruptly.

'I want things back the way they were.' She was suddenly too emotional to guard what she was saying.

'Then you should have thought twice before cheating on me,' Vito grated.

'I never cheated on you!' Lily cried. 'But it doesn't make any difference now.'

'Of course it does—it changed everything!' Vito said.

'But our relationship… Nothing was how it seemed anyway.' She felt tears prick her eyes revealingly, and she looked down so that he wouldn't see. 'You weren't the man I thought you were, or you would never have believed lies about me. You would never have accused me so horribly of something I didn't do.'

She turned away and stared out of the window, but instead she saw her reflection staring back—wide eyed and lost, wearing a crumpled linen suit. Her hair was escaping in wild curls from the tightly pulled-back style she'd tried to impose on it that morning, when she hadn't had time to do it properly—but there was nothing she could do to fix that now. She smoothed her hands automatically over her creased jacket, then took a deep, steadying breath before turning back to face him.

'I'm leaving now.' She was proud at how level her voice sounded, despite the turmoil she was feeling inside.

'No. You're not leaving.' Vito's voice was cold as stone. 'You haven't thought this through yet.'

'There's nothing to think about,' Lily said. 'You've made it very clear what your opinion of me is. Why would I marry you?'

'For your child's sake,' he said. 'Do you want your child to grow up illegitimate? Without a father?' He walked forward and put his hands on her upper arms, holding her in place to emphasise the importance of his words. 'Do you want your baby to be somebody's *dirty little secret*?'

Lily stood stock-still and stared up at Vito. A horrible feeling of nausea was rising up through her, and his hands felt like cold inhuman restraints.

'Why would you say such a horrible thing?' Her voice trembled with emotion as she spoke. Vito's words were too close to the bone. Too close to her own insecurities about her childhood.

'Because *you* know what that would be like for your child,' he said. 'All your life, you've known what it's like to be Reggie Morton's dirty little secret.'

She stared at Vito in horror.

For a moment she forgot to breathe. Her heart forgot to beat.

Then all at once she had to escape—get out of there as fast as she could. She whirled away from Vito automatically, her hands flying up in alarm as she swayed against the window.

Her mind was spinning as her gaze plummeted dizzyingly down into the street far below. They were so high up that nothing looked real—tiny stick-figures, toy cars and model trees were hazy images that were almost out of sight. It was like she was in some kind of awful nightmare.

Then suddenly her vision blurred and she felt herself start to fall into blackness.

'Lily!'

Vito's voice cut through the haze, dragging her back to the harsh reality of her situation. Hands like steel gripped her arms to prevent her from falling, then virtually lifted her away to the huge leather chair by the desk.

'Lily.' Vito dropped down onto one knee in front of her. For a moment she almost made the mistake of thinking he was concerned about her—then as her eyes came into focus she saw that his expression was just as cold as before. He had simply adopted the best position to get a good look at her. And probably to make sure she was looking at him, paying proper attention to what he had to say.

'You're extremely pale,' he said. 'Have you eaten today?'

'Of course I'm pale.' Lily spoke through gritted teeth. Her stomach was churning horribly, and she really thought there was a danger that she might be sick. 'I've had a lot of nasty shocks this morning.'

'Have you eaten?' he insisted. 'What would make you feel better?'

'Getting away from you.' She stood up so quickly that Vito rocked back on his heels, but the rapid movement was a mistake. A wave of nausea rolled through her again, and she clung to the desk for support, feeling her head start to spin.

'Sit down,' Vito barked. 'I'm not letting you leave so that you can faint in the street—if you even get that far.'

One hand was on her shoulder, pressing her back into the chair, and the other snatched up the phone on his desk. Lily only half listened as he reeled off a list of instructions—but she understood that he was ordering food and drink.

She closed her eyes, breathing deeply. As much as she thought she hated Vito right then, she couldn't bear to disgrace herself by being sick in front of him. She already felt vulnerable enough, and that would just be the final humiliation on what was already turning out to be the worst day of her life so far.

Only a few minutes seemed to pass before she heard the elevator doors open, followed by Vito's quiet footfall on the thick grey carpet as he returned across the room. She opened her eyes to see him setting a tray down on the desk.

'Drink this,' he instructed, holding out a large glass of iced water.

She took the water silently, unable to speak for a moment, as the memory of him preparing iced water for her on her last day in Venice flashed through her mind. He might not be the tender, concerned lover she had believed him to be—but he still knew what she liked.

In fact, apparently he knew more about her than she had realised, as she thought about the heartless way he had thrown her troubled childhood in her face.

'You snooped into my background.' She looked at him accusingly, expecting to see at least a hint of embarrassment pass across his shuttered features. But there was nothing. He appeared as unmoved as ever.

'Of course I did. You were living with me—a thorough background-check was mandatory.' His voice was matter-of-fact. 'You had potential access to all kinds of sensitive material.'

Lily looked at him in disgust. It would never have occurred to her to pry into his life like that. She knew he'd been married before; that was common knowledge. But she'd never poked around, trying to discover why his marriage had ended.

'Perhaps I should have run a background-check on you.' Lily took a sip of icy-cold water. It was making her stomach feel a little better—but the rest of her was still a mess of unpleasant emotions. 'I might have found out in time what kind of man I was getting involved with.'

She pushed a coil of blonde hair out of her eyes and looked away from him distractedly. She couldn't believe how things were turning out, and her mind was a horrible whirl of conflicting thoughts.

She should never have come to L&G Enterprises that morning. She'd known Vito held controlling shares in the company. But he also had many other business interests in London. She'd thought, if he was even in the city, what were the chances that he'd be right there in the building? That he'd walk into her presentation?

Maybe a tiny part of her deep down inside had longed to see him again, despite the unforgivable way he had treated her, but she could never have guessed that things would end up like this. That Vito, the man she'd once foolishly believed she was falling in love with, would rub her nose in the humiliating misery of her childhood. And then propose to her.

'Being someone's dirty little secret is not a pleasant position to be in.' Vito's voice was cold and unfeeling as he broke the silence. 'Don't make your child suffer the same fate. You don't need to make the same choices as your mother.'

'You're the one making it dirty!' Lily responded hotly, her gaze flashing back to his impossibly inexpressive face. 'And leave my mother out of it—she's happy living in the countryside, working with the hospice patients.'

'But you're not happy,' Vito said blandly. 'And your childhood was far from happy.'

'You don't know anything about my childhood,' Lily threw back at him.

'I know that your father refused to acknowledge you,' he said. 'That he paid your mother off to keep her quiet. That you've never met him or your two half-sisters, and that it seems unlikely that you ever will. Unless you're prepared to let your mother lose her home and income, just to satisfy your curiosity about the man who didn't want you.'

'Why would I want to meet my father?' Lily responded automatically, despite the way she was reeling under the onslaught of Vito's words. 'He's nothing to me.'

'You mean *you're* nothing to *him*.'

Vito turned away to select a Danish pastry from the tray on his desk. Lily gripped her glass of iced water dangerously tightly and stared at him angrily.

'You are utterly vile,' she said, looking at the plate in his hand, because suddenly she couldn't bring herself to meet his gaze.

How could he eat at a time like this? Did dishing out heartless comments over something so important to her really mean so little to him that he thought he'd combine it with a light snack?

She'd spent a lifetime trying not to think about the way her father had discarded her. And she didn't want to think about it now. She could have searched for him, tried to make him acknowledge her. But she'd always known no good would have come of that. And, in any case, she would never, ever have done anything to cause her mother distress.

'Here, eat this.' Vito removed the glass of water from

her grip and handed her the pastry on a highly glazed black plate. So it hadn't been for him after all.

'I'm not hungry,' Lily said mutinously, trying to pass the plate back.

'Nevertheless, you must eat,' Vito said. 'You'll feel better if you boost your blood-sugar level. You really are exceptionally pale, even for you.'

'Even for me?' Lily snapped. 'Don't act like you know me. You may know my secret—a way you can coerce me into doing what you want. But that's not really knowing someone.'

'It's not coercion,' Vito said. 'I'm merely helping you to recognise the full implications of trying to go it alone with an illegitimate child. In fact, it's more of a reminder, really—after all, you know from first-hand experience what it can be like.'

'It wasn't as bad as you're making it sound,' Lily protested. But in her heart she knew it had been pretty tough—constantly dealing with her mother's depression and her own sense of abandonment and disappointment. She hated the thought of her baby growing up without a father, feeling unwanted and worthless.

'Don't you want to protect your child?' Vito asked. 'Marry me, and he or she will be free of the misery that blighted your childhood.'

'My childhood wasn't miserable,' Lily insisted. She could hear the doubt in her own voice, but suddenly it felt disloyal to her mum even to let herself think it.

'As my heir, your baby will have every opportunity,' Vito continued. 'And you won't experience the difficulties that your mother faced on her own.'

'I don't know,' Lily said. Vito's proposal was totally unexpected and overwhelming. She didn't know what to think any more. 'I don't know what to say.'

Two months ago she would have been unimaginably happy to have Vito propose to her. Now things were different. It was clear he didn't love her. He didn't even trust her. But he was offering her a chance for her child—and wasn't that the most important thing to consider now?

How could she deny her child the life Vito could give it?

'You do know what to say,' Vito said. 'You must agree to marry me. And, in the circumstances, we must arrange the wedding for as soon as possible. We'll fly back to Venice this afternoon.'

He looked at her, sitting so stiffly on the high-backed leather chair, and he thought that she had been right when she'd said he didn't know her. He didn't. The sweet, innocent girl he'd thought she was would never have taken a lover and then tried to pass off another man's child as his.

She didn't even look the same as the eager yet tentative lover he had shared his home with for nearly half a year. Her defensive body-language was completely new to him, and the amount of weight she'd lost made her appear all bony angles beneath her ill-fitting linen suit.

The dark smudges of exhaustion beneath her hazel eyes emphasised their size, making them look extremely large in her painfully thin face. And she was wearing her hair in a strange style that all through their five months together he had never before seen.

But, even though her appearance had changed, the powerful attraction he felt for her had not diminished one jot.

It was the same as the first time he'd laid eyes on her; she'd been standing up in front of another group of executives in another of his companies, pitching an earlier version of the computer software she'd been selling today. He'd walked into that meeting too—with no thought in his head other than the fact that he *must* find out who she was.

It had suddenly been imperative that he invited her to dinner, got to know her…took her to bed.

And the urgent desire that had stormed his body back then was still surging through his veins like molten lava.

He wanted to haul her to her feet and kiss her until the rigid tension in her body melted away. He knew it would—he'd felt the way she'd responded to him earlier. Despite her protests he knew she still wanted him as much as he wanted her.

He wanted to run his hands all over her body, until she was soft and pliant against him. He wanted to release the clip at the nape of her neck and let her hair fly out in crazy curls. It had been only at the end of their most passionate love-making sessions that he'd seen her hair in its natural, untamed state. She'd always spent ages straightening it and smoothing it down into sleek, sophisticated styles. He liked it when it was wild. It made him think of rampant sex.

'Even if I agree, I can't be ready to travel this afternoon.' Lily's voice startled him out of his thoughts. 'There are things I must do, people I have to tell.'

'Of course you can be ready. Leave all the technical details to me. Once we arrive in Venice, you may call anyone you need, to inform them of your change of address.'

Vito suppressed a grim smile of satisfaction at her imminent agreement. He hadn't allowed himself to consider the possibility that she might refuse his offer of marriage.

The fact that she had been unfaithful to him, and

subsequently denied it, had proved him very wrong in his original assessment of her personality. However, he did know what her childhood had been like. And he was confident that his frank reminders of how their uncertain situation had impacted on Lily and her mother would be enough to bring her round to accepting his proposal.

He knew he'd hurt her feelings when he'd thrown her out, but he was sure her maternal instinct to protect her child's future would win out in the end.

'No, I need to—' Lily began.

'Presumably the equipment you brought with you for your presentation belongs to the company you were working for.' Vito picked up the phone to make a call. 'I'll have it returned by courier.'

He had her in his grasp. All that was left to do was to make the arrangements as quickly as possible. Then he would tell his grandfather the news the old man had been hoping to hear for years: the Salvatore family name was to continue.

His grandfather would end his days happy, believing there was a new Salvatore heir. Then afterwards, when Lily was no longer of any use to him, Vito would exact revenge on her by ridding himself of her. And the baby.

A swift divorce, and his life would soon be back to normal. Lily, and the proof of her infidelity, would no longer have any part of it.

'But I can't just disappear off to Italy,' Lily said. 'People will worry about me.'

'A short announcement that we are reunited and about to be married should deal with that,' Vito replied.

'They'll never believe it,' Lily said, wondering how her independent friend, Anna, would react to her decision to marry Vito purely to ensure security and stability for her child. How would she explain that she couldn't bear the thought of her baby enduring a childhood as tough as hers? 'Everyone knows how badly you treated me—they won't be fooled by any story I tell them.'

Or at least Anna wouldn't, she thought. Somehow she'd never really got round to telling her mother any details about how she came to be back in London.

'No.' The word cut through the air like steel. 'No one must ever know this is anything other than a normal marriage.'

'But...' Lily faltered as he took her hands and pulled her abruptly to her feet. She was standing directly in front of him, and she could feel the intensity radiating off him. Her heart jolted nervously in her chest. He was utterly serious.

'*No one* will ever know.' Vito's voice throbbed and his eyes blazed. 'You will make them all believe that it is a normal marriage, that the child you are carrying is mine. If you fail to do this, I will cast you and the baby out.'

Lily stared at him numbly.

She just couldn't let her baby go through what she had experienced growing up. Vito's words 'dirty little secret' rang in her mind. He had been agonisingly accurate in his assessment of what her childhood had been like.

Living with a mother who was depressed and frequently plagued by worries and self-doubts had been tough. Having very little money, no father figure at home, and, on top of everything else, dealing with spiteful taunts from other children had been a constant grind.

But realising that her own father didn't want to meet her—probably wished she'd never even been born—had quite simply been heartbreaking. She couldn't let her child grow up never knowing its father—and she knew for sure that this baby was Vito's.

She had to agree. For the sake of her unborn baby she had to agree to marry Vito.

CHAPTER FOUR

LILY placed the large vase of blue cornflowers on the table. She put her handwritten note to Anna beside them and stood back, biting her lip in consternation.

She didn't want to disappear out of her friend's life as abruptly as she'd arrived, but she had a plane to catch, and couldn't be there to explain in person. Besides, she had a terrible fear that if she talked to her friend face to face she would almost certainly break down and tell her everything. The future of her unborn baby depended on her playing out the charade that Vito was demanding. She couldn't allow herself to fall at the first hurdle.

The cornflowers were gorgeous, and she knew they were Anna's favourites. She'd spotted them outside a florist on the way back to the flat, and decided at once that she must buy a huge bunch for her friend.

Vito's driver had tried to pay for them, but Lily was having none of that. From her time in Venice she was used to his assistants popping up beside her, cash or credit card in hand. But these flowers were a gift for a dear friend, a friend who'd been there for her in a time of trouble. She wasn't going to let it be sullied by allowing Vito to pay for it. She might have agreed to marry him, but she wasn't letting him buy her off.

Lily looked round the flat that had been her home for six weeks. It wasn't really home, but she'd been so grateful for Anna's comforting presence. There would be no one to comfort her in Venice.

It hadn't taken her long to pack—she'd been travelling light since leaving Venice. She turned away and started carrying her bags down to the waiting limousine. The driver hurried to help her, and in hardly any time her belongings were stowed in the boot.

She stood on the pavement, staring at the keys in her hand, suddenly reluctant to go despite the fact that she must.

'Would you like me to take them?' the driver politely enquired. 'Is there a trusted neighbour I can leave them with? Or should I drop them through the letter box?'

Lily blinked and stared at him for a moment. All of Vito's staff were honest and ready to help with anything. But this was a task she had to do herself.

'No, thank you.' Lily smiled at him as warmly as she could, but she knew it couldn't look very convincing. She was utterly exhausted and felt sick to her stomach. 'I'll just be a moment.'

She made her way wearily back up the two flights of stairs and let herself into the flat one last time. She placed the keys on the table next to her note and the vase of cornflowers, then walked back out and pulled the door shut behind her. She pushed it automatically, just to check the lock had caught, and suddenly she felt locked out of her own life. As her fingers fell from the unyielding door, she knew she was saying goodbye to her freedom.

A few hours later she was sitting next to Vito as their plane circled the city of Venice, coming in to land across the water at the edge of the lagoon. It looked so different from the city she had flown away from six weeks ago, the day after she'd told Vito she was pregnant. By morning most of the fog had lifted, allowing the airport to reopen, but the city had still looked eerily colourless, and the wide expanse of water had been a pale, metallic grey.

Now the sun was shining brightly, low in the western sky, and the water of the lagoon was a luxuriant blue, tinged with the gold of the approaching sunset. The island of Venice itself looked amazing from the air—like a perfect miniature replica dropped into the open space of the lagoon. Famous landmarks stood out with incredible clarity, and for a moment Lily almost felt like she'd never left. Except now everything was different.

'Do you feel well enough to walk down to the water?' She heard Vito speak beside her, and she turned to look at him in surprise. It really wasn't very far down to the pier where his personal boat would be waiting for them. They'd always made their way on foot in the past.

'I'd like to walk,' she replied. 'Thank you for asking.' She was still wearing the high-heeled shoes she'd worn for her presentation, and her feet were starting to ache, but after the flight she could definitely do with some fresh air.

It wasn't long before they were zipping across the water towards the city. Lily loved being out on the lagoon, and she'd always been entranced by the idea that she was travelling across the water to arrive at the city in the same way people had for more than a thousand years. Then, all too soon, they were winding their way through the maze of Venetian canals, approaching the water gate of Vito's gothic *palazzo*.

She couldn't help remembering the last time she'd disembarked there. That afternoon the fog had chilled her to the bone, and she'd been worried how Vito would react to her pregnancy. But despite everything she had been optimistic. She could never have predicted the harsh and unfathomable way he would react, initially throwing her out, and then persuading her to return with him to become his wife for reasons she still didn't fully understand.

She climbed out onto the marble steps soberly. Leaving this *palazzo* and her life with Vito had been devastating—but returning under such circumstances was equally hard.

'No doubt you'll want to rest this evening.' Vito guided Lily towards the stairs as several members of staff appeared to carry her belongings.

'I think that would be best,' Lily responded, suddenly feeling tears prick behind her eyes. Coming back to the place where she'd been so happy was affecting her more than she had expected.

Vito took her up to the grand bedroom she had previously shared with him, then left without saying a word.

For a moment she stood rooted to the spot, looking round at the room that was so familiar, yet seemed so strange. Then, taking a deep breath, she walked purposefully across to her luggage to find her wash-kit and nightclothes.

She was tired and emotional, but she wouldn't give in to it. She wouldn't let herself think about what she had got herself into. Vito had made her play his game, but she was going to remain strong and positive. She would not let him see any vulnerability.

She reached up and released her hair from the clip at the back of her head. It had been uncomfortable on the plane, but she'd been reluctant to let her hair down in front of Vito. She walked through to the *en suite* to take a quick shower and get ready for bed.

Although it was dark outside now, it wasn't really

very late. But pregnancy and the stresses of the day had made Lily so tired that she longed for sleep. She had no doubt that Vito would join her later, but with any luck she'd be sound asleep before he made an appearance.

Lily was alone in the bed when she awoke the following morning. She gazed up at the beautiful painted ceiling and the antique Murano glass chandelier, realising that she'd actually slept very well. And, more importantly, she felt better than she had for days. Maybe her morning sickness was finally starting to ease.

She sat up cautiously, noticing a glass of iced water had been placed on her bedside table. Beaded with condensation, the water looked enticingly cool, and next to it someone had left a plate of her favourite sweet rolls from a local bakery.

She smiled grimly. Eating before she showered and dressed would help to keep her stomach settled, but it bugged her that for some reason Vito was still demonstrating how well he thought he knew her, and how he understood her condition. She picked up the glass and took a refreshing sip, rebelliously thinking that perhaps she should inform him that her new preference was cold milk.

She'd just finished one of the rolls when the door opened and Vito walked in.

As usual he looked absolutely amazing, and was immaculately groomed, right down to his freshly buffed handmade leather shoes. He was wearing smart trousers and a black cashmere sweater that fitted him perfectly. Somehow the luxuriously soft layer of wool encasing his hard, muscled form emphasised his raw masculine power in a way that made her heart skip a beat.

Lily remembered what it felt like to be enfolded in

his arms and held against that sweater. She pushed the thought aside and lifted her eyes to his handsome face.

'Good, you're awake.' He stood at the foot of the bed, letting his eyes run over her in assessment. 'You look much better than yesterday.'

'It's not surprising.' She returned his gaze steadily, resisting the urge to fidget under his hard stare. She was glad that she was wearing her old, cosy nightshirt with long sleeves and a high neckline. Vito had always hated it. He'd preferred her in the filmy, revealing garments he had seemed to enjoy buying for her. 'Yesterday was just about the worst day of my life.'

'There's someone you need to meet this morning,' he said, ignoring her jibe. 'My grandfather has been ill. A visit from us will cheer him up.'

Lily looked at him in startled silence. She'd lived with Vito for five months, but he had never once taken her to visit his grandfather. She'd known that he lived very nearby, and that Vito called in to see him regularly. But she'd understood that, as his lover, it was not part of her role to meet his family.

'You intend to tell him, don't you?' She found her voice at last, the realisation that everything was so different making her feel really unsettled.

'Of course, he's my grandfather. I didn't bring you here to marry you in secret,' Vito replied. 'I thought I made myself very plain on that point.'

'You did,' Lily said. 'It's just that it was rather a sudden decision. I thought you might take time to reflect on it before things get too complicated to change.' She folded her arms across her chest, thinking that, once other people knew about their marriage, there would definitely be no going back.

'The decision has been made,' Vito said. 'All that

remains is to tell those who are important to us, and to start the ball rolling with the preparations for our wedding. As I said yesterday, it will be at the earliest opportunity.'

Lily looked away from him, knocked for six by the thought of actually telling people that she was getting married. Her note to Anna certainly hadn't gone into details like that. She knew her friend would have found such a sudden announcement bewildering, especially after the way Vito had callously thrown her out.

She didn't want Anna to worry about her, so she'd kept the message simple and upbeat—just saying she'd run into Vito, they'd patched things up between them, and she was returning to Venice with him.

If she was getting married she ought to tell her mother, but she honestly couldn't bear the thought of sharing her news with her mother, or anyone else she was close to. Although she knew she had to go through with it because it was the best thing for her child, she still had misgivings about the way Vito had treated her. About the way he was continuing to treat her.

How would she manage to keep up the pretence that it was a perfectly normal, happy marriage in front of people who knew her well and cared about her? She simply couldn't afford to reveal the truth behind the marriage. Vito had made it plain that they must maintain a normal happily-married front. Her child's future depended on it.

'We'll leave as soon as you're ready,' Vito said, walking to the door. 'My grandfather is at his best in the morning. He tends to sleep in the afternoon.'

Lily pushed back the covers, got out of bed and headed for the *en suite*. Half an hour later, she was sitting at the dressing table, adding the finishing touches to her make-up while she waited for Vito to return.

She was apprehensive about meeting his grandfather, and had tried to ease her nerves by taking extra care with her appearance. Her hair was freshly washed and straightened, so that it hung down in a sleek blonde curtain well past her shoulder blades. Her make-up was light and natural looking, but the judicious use of blusher had given her a bit of colour in her cheeks.

She had chosen to wear her ivory linen-suit again. It was a bit creased from travelling, but everything else was still packed haphazardly in her bags and was not likely to look any better. She looked in the mirror and decided that, although she might not look very glamorous, she was perfectly presentable.

The door opened and Vito came into the room.

'I'm ready to go,' she said, standing up quickly and reaching for her handbag.

Vito looked at her, picking up small details that were different from the day before. She didn't look so washed-out and, with her hair brushed down in that shimmering veil halfway down her back, she was starting to look more like the beautiful young woman he'd shared his life with over the winter. But she was still wearing the ill-fitting suit from the day before.

'I know this outfit isn't perfect,' Lily said, as if she'd read his mind. Or maybe, he thought, she'd simply read his expression. Although her shocking act of betrayal had made her a stranger to him, he mustn't forget that they'd lived together for five months. Undoubtedly she'd got to know him quite well in that time. 'But I don't have anything else suitable,' she added.

'A dress would be better.' Vito turned to open the huge fitted-wardrobe on her side of the room. 'Preferably something with a bit of colour—to brighten my grandfather's morning.'

'But…' Lily stared into the wardrobe in obvious surprise. 'All my clothes.'

'You didn't take them with you.'

Vito selected a soft peach-coloured silk dress he had bought for her in Milan. Lily was always drawn towards natural, pale colours—her favourites were cream and ivory—and, despite the fact he knew they suited her, he'd always had the urge to liven up her choices. 'I had to assume none of the items I bought for you were to your taste after all,' he added.

'I didn't pay for any of them,' Lily said. 'They were all so expensive—I didn't think they were mine to take.'

'Of course they were.' Vito suddenly felt annoyed. He'd enjoyed buying things for her, and when he'd seen she'd left them behind it had been a brutal reminder of how she'd duped him—like a spiteful smack on the cheek, on top of her shameless infidelity. 'What did you think *I* was going to do with them?'

'I don't know,' Lily said, smoothing her hand over her hair in a gesture that revealed how unsettled she felt. 'Maybe sell them. Or give them away. I never expected to find them still in the wardrobe.'

Vito turned and looked at her, deliberately keeping his expression bland as he laid the peach dress out on the bed. He wouldn't let himself think too closely about why he'd never got rid of all the things she'd left in his room.

Over the years he had invited very few women to share his home. And, once he had decided it was over, it was over—completely. For the most part they had taken everything with them, especially anything of value, like designer clothes and jewellery. Then any remaining items had been disposed of quickly, eradicating any evidence that anyone had ever been in his home.

But when his housekeeper had enquired about Lily's

belongings, he had barked at her to leave them. After that the poor woman hadn't mentioned them again—and had left them well alone. Out of sight in wardrobes and cupboards. But not entirely out of mind.

'You left the clothes and the jewellery,' he said. 'But you were quick enough to take every last piece of the lingerie I bought for you.'

'The clothes, the jewellery—they cost so much,' Lily said. A pretty flush had risen to her heart-shaped face, making the blood flow faster around Vito's body.

'The lingerie was expensive too.' He took a step closer to her, getting a kick of satisfaction as she refused to back away, even though he had clearly invaded her personal space. 'You knew that.'

'What would you want with my lingerie?' A spark in her hazel eyes and a defiant lift to her chin challenged him. 'Even you wouldn't sell second-hand underclothes.'

'I didn't want to sell them,' Vito said, deliberately letting his voice drop to a seductive purr. 'I wanted them for myself. You were gone, the nights were long…'

Lily gasped, suddenly speechless as she stared at his handsome face. 'Don't be so…so…'

'Don't looked shocked. It's a natural desire. You know how good we were together…*physically*,' Vito said. 'There's nothing wrong with wanting something to remember you by.'

'Stop it,' Lily said, hearing an edge of panic in her tone. But Vito's voice was rumbling through her, making her remember what it had been like to make love with him.

'I wanted to hold the flimsy little things in my hand as I thought about the good times we'd spent together,' he drawled, with blatant come-to-bed eyes locked onto hers from under sultry, half-closed lids. 'I longed to smooth the silky fabric against my skin—thinking about the feel of your skin against mine.'

'Stop it.' Lily's cheeks were starting to burn. 'You could have gone out and bought some more lingerie if you were so desperate.'

'It wouldn't have been the same,' Vito replied, with a meaningful smile on his full, sensual lips. 'It was knowing that the silk had been next to your body, pressing close to your most intimate places…'

Lily bit her lip, trying to think of a suitably cutting remark to put a stop to this line of discussion. She wasn't used to Vito talking like this, but although it was unsettling there was also something strangely exciting about it.

A wave of warmth was washing through her body, putting her senses onto full alert in a way that hadn't happened since she'd left Venice, until yesterday in Vito's empty penthouse.

'Are you wearing something I bought you now?' Vito's eyes were running over her, as if with his X-ray vision he could see through her linen suit to discover what underwear she had chosen. 'Or have you discarded it all—along with the sanctity of our relationship?'

'It's none of your business what I'm wearing under my suit,' Lily said, appalled by how her breath was catching in her throat.

'It used to be my business.' Vito dropped to his knees beside her and placed his large, warm hands on her hips. He tugged her gently towards him so that his cheek was resting on her stomach. 'You used to like me to come home from work, take you in my arms and hold you close. You loved it when I ran my hands up your legs, slipped them under your skirt, and traced my fingers over the silk and lace that covered the most sensitive part of your body.'

'That's over now.' Lily struggled to keep her voice level as Vito's words set off an alarming chain-reaction of sensation through her. It was true that she had loved the touch of his hands on her body, had revelled in the way that he made her feel. 'That was before you treated me so horribly.'

'Yes,' Vito said, letting his hands start to slide slowly down over her hips and thighs. 'That time is over. But now we are starting a different stage in our relationship. We are soon to be man and wife.'

Lily stood absolutely still, acutely aware of the movement of his hands. The familiarity of his touch was triggering a mass of conflicting feelings in her. Her body knew him, knew what exquisite pleasure he could give her.

But her heart felt betrayed. How could she be responding to him after he had treated her so unforgivably?

'It won't be the same,' she said, thinking how special it had been to make love to him when she'd believed he cared about her. She'd always thought it was more than just sex.

'It will be better.' Suddenly his fingers were unzipping her skirt. 'It will be the cement that holds our marriage together. Neither of us wants this marriage to fail—there is too much at stake.'

Lily's heart skipped a beat as her skirt slipped to the floor. Part of her wanted to flee to the *en suite* and cover up with a warm, fluffy robe. But most of her was shamelessly enjoying the feel of Vito's eyes as he ran his gaze over the French lace-knickers she was wearing.

'Are you wearing the matching bra?' He stood up and started unbuttoning the front of her jacket.

It was almost impossible for Lily to stand still. Liquid desire was running through her veins, making her feel more alive than she could remember. It was as if she had merely been existing, waiting to be back in Vito's arms.

Since he had stormed back into her life, demanding that she marry him, she'd known that this moment was inevitable. He was a red-blooded male, with a powerful libido. Celibacy was not in his nature. If this marriage was to succeed, then sex would play an important part.

But his hands were moving so slowly. It was taking him too long to remove her clothes. She yearned to feel his hands on her body, to feel his naked skin next to hers. She ached for him to make love to her, because that was surely what was to follow. And then she could let herself pretend that things were back to normal—that he had never thrown her out, and the last six weeks had never happened.

At last her jacket fell away to reveal a plain stretch-lace camisole. He took hold of the hem and pulled it over her head. Then he stepped back and let his gaze slide all over her.

Lily stood in her lacy bra and French knickers, still wearing her hold-up stockings and high-heeled shoes. Hot anticipation pooled deep inside her. Her breasts felt heavy, and her nipples were diamond-hard points straining against the flimsy covering of lace.

He'd hardly touched her, yet a sensual tingle moved through her body, settling in her most intimate place, making her need for him almost unbearable. She could feel her exposed skin flushing, betraying her sexual readiness to him.

His blue eyes grew darker as he looked at her, and she knew exactly how the sight of her was affecting him. She could hear the change in his breathing, recognise the expression on his face that meant he wanted to make love to her. But he made no move towards her.

Suddenly a shuttered look descended over his features and he turned to pick up the peach dress from the bed.

'You've lost weight,' he said. 'But this style should be forgiving.'

'*Forgiving?*'

His choice of word was like a slap in the face.

At that exact moment she knew he would never forgive her for what he *thought* she'd done. It made no difference that he was mistaken, that there was no possible proof of her sin against him—her denial would continue to fall on deaf ears.

'You are the one that needs forgiveness, for the awful way you treated me. For the way you're still treating me!' She snatched her clothes up off the floor and held them protectively across her body.

He had never truly planned to make love to her. His intention that morning had only ever been to humiliate her.

But she'd spoken her mind before she thought about the consequences, and as Vito turned back towards her his fury was almost palpable.

'Don't pursue this.' His words were forced out through gritted teeth, and she could see the monumental effort he was exerting to control his rage. 'You won't win. You *can't* win. It would be better for everyone if you don't keep reminding me of your betrayal—of the fact that you are carrying another man's child inside you.'

'But—'

Vito didn't need to speak again to quell Lily's retort. As his gaze met hers, the tortured look in his eyes cut through her pain, and in a sudden instant of clarity she realised how he was being torn apart by his belief that she had cheated on him.

But it wasn't her fault that he thought she'd been unfaithful. Was it madness to stay with someone who thought her capable of such a thing? But she'd made her decision—she had to marry him to make a future for her unborn child.

Later, for her own sake, she was going to have to try to discover why he believed what he did. But for now she had to let it rest. From the anger and tension radiating from every ounce of his powerful body, she could tell that now was not the time to keep pushing him. There was no chance of having a reasoned conversation with him while he was so tightly wound and his anger so raw.

'Put this on,' Vito said, holding out the dress to her.

She slipped it over her head silently, gathered her long hair to one side, and turned to present him with the zip. She straightened her shoulders consciously, determined to show him that her will was as strong as his. She wouldn't fight with him now—but neither would she let herself be quashed by the brute strength of his personality.

He pulled the zip up slowly, not touching her at all. She exhaled quietly, careful not to let him know that she'd been holding her breath in case his fingers brushed against her sensitive spine. Then she turned to look at her reflection in the mirror.

She hardly recognised the girl who gazed back at her. The girl who'd worn that dress and lived in this bedroom— *that* girl—belonged to another time. A happier time.

If she was going to survive this marriage, she was going to have to assert herself. Show Vito that, despite his threats and undeniable position of strength, he couldn't walk all over her.

'That will do very well,' Vito said, his patronising tone setting Lily's nerves on edge. He passed her bag to her and headed towards the door. 'We must set off to my grandfather's.'

'Wait a minute.' Lily gripped her suede bag tightly and dug in her heels.

'What is it?' Vito turned back impatiently.

'That sweater,' she said, tossing her bag onto the bed and walking briskly towards him. 'It's not right. You can't wear a depressing black sweater if you're serious about cheering your grandfather up.'

'He won't be looking at *me*…' Vito's words petered out as she gripped the soft cashmere in her hands and started peeling it off his body.

'You must have something lighter and fresher. Maybe your pale-blue sweater?' It was an effort to keep her voice steady, but she was proud of how matter-of-fact she managed to sound. Especially when she discovered he wasn't wearing anything under the sweater, and an intoxicating waft of his pure, masculine aroma filled her senses, making her legs feel weak all over again.

She took a step back, and for a second let her eyes run over his magnificent form. A shiver of sensual appreciation ran through her, and she realised her ploy to regain some control was in serious danger of backfiring on her.

Vito turned and stepped towards his wardrobe. Try as she might, she simply couldn't tear her gaze away. She'd always loved to watch him without his shirt on—never failing to be fascinated, and frankly turned on, by the irresistible play of his well-defined muscles beneath his golden-brown skin.

'It's your choice.' He indicated the neatly folded piles of sweaters in his wardrobe—but for a moment Lily got the impression he wasn't simply talking about clothing. He'd seen the way she was looking at him. He knew how she was reacting.

Was he letting her know that, if she was prepared to

make the first move, he wanted to make love to her after all?

With an effort of will, she pushed the thought aside. He was probably playing with her again, and she certainly didn't intend to cause herself any more humiliation.

'This is a cheerful colour,' she said, tossing a blue sweater at him. 'That will brighten your grandfather's day.'

Vito pulled it on silently. Then, without even bothering to check his appearance in the mirror, took her hand and pulled her towards the door.

CHAPTER FIVE

CA' SALVATORE, the beautiful *palazzo* that had been the home of Giovanni Salvatore for more than seventy-five years, stood in the very heart of the city on a magnificent stretch of the Grand Canal.

It was possible to make the journey from Vito's home by water, using the impressive canal entrances of both *palazzi*, but Lily was pleased when he decided they should walk. She had missed strolling through the maze of narrow streets, along canals and over bridges. Although she had lived in Venice for quite a while, she'd discovered something new almost every outing, and had always taken pleasure from investigating unfamiliar areas.

Now she walked apprehensively beside Vito. He'd told her that his grandfather was old and frail, but she knew that for most of his life Giovanni had been a formidable Venetian businessman. Vito had often spoken of him with a great deal of respect, but also great love.

She knew that when Vito was a child he'd come to live with his grandfather at *Ca' Salvatore* after his parents had died in an accident. It was clear that Giovanni was still hugely important to him—as was this visit. For everyone's sake, she hoped things would go smoothly.

It didn't take long to reach the baroque *palazzo*, and for a moment Lily gazed in awe at the building's amazing façade, complete with marble pillars and statues.

'And this is just the back entrance.' Vito paused beside her to look up at the bold ornamentation. 'The side facing the canal is really something to behold.'

Lily smiled in surprise at his tone. He'd grown up in this grand historic palace, but he didn't take it for granted, and was obviously very proud of his family's heritage. She glanced sideways at him, and for a moment he looked like the Vito she used to know. He appeared relaxed and almost happy—as if coming to *Ca' Salvatore* was like coming home for him. Suddenly she had the feeling that he was genuinely looking forward to seeing his grandfather and telling him their news.

He took her hand in his. It was a gesture that could be taken equally as a sign of possession or affection, and once more she was reminded how important it was that she played her part well. He led her into the building and up to the second-floor room where the housekeeper had told them Giovanni was resting in bed.

The moment they entered the old man's bedchamber, Lily got a sense that something wasn't right. Vito stiffened beside her the instant he laid eyes on his grandfather, then he dropped her hand and crossed to the bed in two long strides.

'*Nonno?*' Vito bent down to speak close to his grandfather's ear. 'Are you feeling all right?'

Lily stood beside the door, not sure what to do. The housekeeper had said Giovanni was resting, but she hadn't implied that anything was wrong. And, from Lily's perspective, she couldn't identify what had made Vito react so strongly. Giovanni looked old and tired, but maybe Vito had spotted something more worrying in his appearance because he knew him so well.

'Vito?' The old man's voice was weak, but he was looking at his grandson's face with recognition. 'I'm tired, that's all.'

'I'm calling the doctor,' Vito said. 'I don't like the way you look.'

'Hmph!' Giovanni snorted. 'You don't have to like the way I look—I'm not one of your women.'

Lily smiled at the old man's quick humour. His comment on Vito's women was unsettling—but he clearly had his wits about him. And it was obvious that, even though he appeared to be bed-bound, he was still a man to be reckoned with.

Vito was leaning close, talking to his grandfather in a firm but kind voice. It was plain from his body language and tone of voice that the old man meant the world to him.

Suddenly Lily's throat felt tight, and a foolish tear sprang to her eye as she remembered Vito talking to her in a gentle and caring way. But he wasn't like that with her any more. She blinked and turned away, trying not to think about just how different things were between them now.

She looked around the chamber to distract herself, running her gaze over the impressively frescoed walls with admiration. The ornate decoration in the chamber was truly splendid—fitting for the main bedchamber of an important *palazzo* on the Grand Canal.

It was incredible to think that this was Giovanni's bedroom. The chamber wouldn't have looked out of place in one of the many magnificent Venetian palaces open to the public. And the fact that she could see no evidence of modern technological living made it even more like stepping back in time to a more elegant age.

A movement caught her eye, and she turned to see Vito striding towards her. Before she knew what he was doing, he took her arm and hustled her out into the hallway.

'Now is not a good time for you to meet my grandfather,' he said, guiding her towards the grand staircase.

'Is there anything I can do to help?' Lily said automatically, although she knew Vito well enough to know he'd already have everything covered.

'No,' he said shortly. 'Go home now. I'll see you later.'

With that he turned on his heel and went back into Giovanni's room, closing the door in her face.

Lily stared after him in consternation. She understood Vito was concerned about his grandfather, but she didn't like the feeling of being so peremptorily dismissed.

She walked slowly down the stairs, thinking again how much things had changed. The old Vito would never have sent her off to find her own way home without an escort. In fact, when she'd first lived with him, it had taken her a long time to persuade him that no harm would come to her if she strolled around the city on her own. No one else had ever showed so much concern for her welfare, and at the time she'd been deeply touched by it.

She headed back to Vito's *palazzo*, strangely surprised by how familiar everything still felt despite the time she'd spent in London. She was almost on autopilot, weaving her way through the maze of narrow lanes without even thinking about her route.

Suddenly she stopped in her tracks right outside a busy *gelateria*. There was no need to go straight back just because Vito had told her to. She should take some time just for herself and try to clear her head.

She joined the queue to buy an ice cream, and a few minutes later she was sitting beside a canal in the late morning sunshine, pleased that her appetite had returned so she could truly enjoy one of her favourite treats.

The steps leading down to the canal were a good place to sit, out of the main flow of pedestrians, and it was restful watching the water lapping against the buildings that edged the other side of the canal.

She ate her ice cream slowly, determined to relish every drop. Then, once she had finished, she let her thoughts return to the predicament she had got herself into with Vito.

Everything had happened so fast since he'd walked in on her presentation yesterday. His proposal had taken her completely by surprise, but in the end she had agreed to marry him for her baby's sake. She'd truly thought it would be best for her child to grow up part of a proper family, with two parents.

Also, deep down inside, she couldn't forget how wonderful things had been between them before he'd thrown her out. Maybe, once they were living together again, things would return to the way they had once been.

But there was a massive problem. For some reason Vito believed she had cheated on him, and that the child she was carrying was not his. That was why he was so angry with her and why he was treating her so harshly.

Lily had no idea what had made him believe this. No matter how hard she thought about it, she couldn't think of anything she had ever said or done that might have led him to that conclusion. There had been nights when they'd been apart, but that had always been because of his business travel. She had never spent a night away from the *palazzo* without Vito.

Suddenly she knew what to do. If she could prove to Vito that she'd never been unfaithful, maybe he would trust her again. Although he'd hurt her feelings with his lack of faith in her, presumably he did have a reason. It would have been better if he'd had the courtesy to tell her, but obviously he was upset by it.

She'd ask him for a paternity test. Then, once he was convinced of the truth, perhaps things could get back to normal between then. That would be best for everyone—for Lily and Vito. And, most importantly, for the baby.

Lily stood up with a burst of energy. She'd found the solution to the problem—soon everything would be all right.

Vito returned to the *palazzo* in the early afternoon. Lily was waiting for him in the bedroom, knowing the conversation she planned to have with him would be best in private. He'd been so concerned that no one should know there was anything untoward about their marriage plans that she thought he wouldn't appreciate her talking to him about paternity tests in a room where a member of staff might overhear.

'How is your grandfather?' she asked, standing up as he walked into the room.

'The doctor thinks he's fine. Well, as fine as he ever is.' From the look on his face it was clear that Vito did not agree. 'I'm not so sure. He doesn't seem right to me,' he said. 'Maybe he's coming down with something.'

'He's lucky to have you nearby,' Lily said. 'I know you'll make sure he receives the best possible care.'

Vito didn't respond. He appeared to be deep in thought as he opened his wardrobe and took out one of his many hand-tailored suits. He must be going straight to the office, Lily thought, realising she'd have to speak fast if she didn't want to lose her opportunity.

He looked so worried about his grandfather that she

longed to comfort him. But she knew she was the last person he would accept comfort from—not while he still believed the worst of her.

She hesitated, knowing it might seem insensitive to bring up paternity testing while Vito was preoccupied with his grandfather's health. But on the other hand, if she could make things right between them, she could be there to help him through his grandfather's illness.

'Vito.' Lily took a deep breath and steeled herself to start a conversation that she knew could be difficult. 'Have you got a few minutes to talk?'

Vito turned to look at her, holding a dark-grey suit on a hanger in his hand, and frowned. The last thing he wanted right then was to talk.

'Make it quick,' he said, laying his suit on the bed and going back to the wardrobe to select a shirt. 'I have a meeting in half an hour.'

'I will be quick,' she said. 'But you have to listen to me properly.'

Vito gritted his teeth and turned to face her. She'd been back in his life less than a day and already she was testing his patience.

'You are upset with me because you think I was unfaithful,' she said, shaking her sleek curtain of blonde hair back over her shoulders.

'Upset?' Vito repeated incredulously, watching her hair swing alluringly as it settled into place. Perhaps she was hoping to distract him with her feminine wiles. 'My God! You English really have mastered the art of understatement.'

'I'm not just going to let your accusation pass,' Lily said. Her voice was calm, but Vito could see her hands were shaking as she gripped them together in front of her.

'I was not unfaithful to you. And I don't know why you think that. I've never done anything to give you that idea.'

Vito stared at her, wondering how she was able to make herself sound so sincere when he knew she was guilty as sin.

'You are right,' he said. 'You covered your trail well. But that doesn't change the fact that I know you betrayed me.'

'I didn't,' Lily protested. 'And the fact that you could even think that about me is just as much of a betrayal. But I don't want to go on like this. I want a paternity test to prove you are my child's father.'

Vito stared at her, feeling tension knot painfully in his stomach. She wanted a paternity test—the one thing he dreaded.

But he'd known it would come to this sooner or later. Although Lily had obviously been sleeping with two men at once, as far as she was concerned it was possible Vito might be the father.

For Lily a paternity test was just a game of chance. There would be a delay until it could be carried out, and she was willing to gamble on the outcome being lucky for her. It was a risk worth taking, because from her point of view she had nothing to lose—he already believed she'd been unfaithful.

But Vito had everything to lose. For him, the test could not produce a good result. There was no way he could win.

He knew he wasn't the father—because he could not have children.

'There will be no paternity test.' Vito clenched his fists at his sides.

He would not allow himself to be subject to physical, public proof that he was not the father of Lily's child. If his grandfather ever found out that the baby was not a true Salvatore heir, it would destroy his happiness for ever.

That was the whole point of marrying Lily. And he had to live with it until the time came when he could discard her and the baby. Even though she continued to show no sign that she had done anything wrong, or take any responsibility for her actions, this was the perfect way for Vito to bring a baby into the family—to make his grandfather happy before he died.

And then there was the other reason he would not submit to a paternity test. The real, gut-wrenching reason that made his palms start to sweat and his blood run cold. He simply could not bear to think of it—he could not face having his inability to father a child thrust in his face again.

'Why not?' Lily demanded. 'Why not have a paternity test and put all this misery behind us?'

'*If* I turned out to be the father, that does not prove your fidelity,' Vito grated.

Only his ex-wife, Capricia, and her fertility expert, knew of his failure as a man. The memory of Capricia's scornful face as she'd waved the doctors report under his nose was almost as painful as his infertility itself.

He would *never* admit his failure to anyone else—especially not to Lily.

'But…' Lily hesitated, looking up at his troubled face. There was something different in his expression, something she hadn't seen before. But she couldn't ponder it for too long. It had been hard enough to make this conversation happen, and it wasn't over yet. She owed it to herself to keep trying to get through to Vito. And he owed it to her to give a proper explanation.

'Where does that leave us?' she continued. 'If we don't have trust—where can we go from here?'

'This isn't about *us*,' Vito said coldly. 'This is about saving your baby from a miserable life as an illegitimate child.'

'But you can't deny me a paternity test then not even tell me why you don't believe me,' Lily insisted. 'How can I defend myself if I don't know what proof you think you have against me?'

'What you've done is indefensible,' Vito said, picking up his suit and shirt and striding towards the door. 'I don't have to give you any more information to weave your web of lies around.'

In a moment he was gone, and Lily was left alone, staring miserably after him. The last two days had been an overwhelming series of shocks, and now she realised she was shaking with reaction to it all.

She sat down on the chair, feeling her hand settle on something soft and warm. Without thinking she picked it up. It was Vito's black cashmere sweater. She lifted it automatically to her face, pressing the luxurious woollen fabric to her skin, and breathed in deeply, inhaling Vito's aroma.

Tears suddenly sprung to her eyes as she remembered the last time she had been enfolded in his embrace while he'd been wearing that sweater. She'd come inside from the foggy city, holding a joyful secret inside her. She'd felt so safe and so secure in his arms—thinking that he cared about her and would protect her from anything.

But it had all been an empty illusion. Five minutes later he had turned on her. And from then on her life had been sucked into a whirlpool of misery, getting increasingly out of her control. And this last argument had been the worst, with Vito not even giving her the information she needed to defend herself.

But she'd had enough. She wouldn't put up with it

any more. She might not be able to fight Vito over his accusation of infidelity. But there was some control she could take. She wasn't going to keep looking back at the special relationship she'd mistakenly believed she'd had with Vito. From now on she was going to concentrate on her future and make the best out of her new life.

She looked down at the black sweater which she was still holding on her lap. It was a harsh reminder of how much her life with Vito had changed—a reminder she did not need.

She stood up decisively and carried the sweater across the room. She opened the window and tossed it out into the canal below.

CHAPTER SIX

'WE'LL eat out tonight,' Vito said. 'To mark your return to Venice.'

'That would be nice.' Lily spoke mildly, determined not to let Vito see she was still shaken from their earlier argument.

It would be good to get out of the *palazzo*. It was less than twenty-four hours since Vito had brought her back to his home, and so far she'd been a bundle of nerves.

It wasn't surprising that she felt on edge after what had happened, nevertheless she'd tried to take her own advice and stop dwelling on it. She'd spent the afternoon pointlessly trying to lose herself in a good book, but even a favourite pastime like reading hadn't distracted her from all the unsettling thoughts that were whirling round persistently inside her head.

'We'll go to Luigi's,' Vito said.

'Oh…I…' Lily drew an anxious breath and stared up at Vito, quickly trying to think of an excuse not to go to Luigi's. After what had happened on Lily's last night in Venice, bringing Vito and Luigi into contact could be risky.

The restaurant had always been one of their favourite places to eat. It was within easy walking distance of the *palazzo*, served some of the best dishes in Venice, and it had a wonderful ambiance. Luigi, the proprietor, was a true character with an expansive personality and a generous nature.

The night Vito had thrown Lily out, Luigi's kindness had been an absolute godsend for her. Trapped in a fogbound city, with every hotel she'd tried full and every mode of transport closed to her, Luigi had literally saved the day. He'd arranged for her to stay in his mother's guest room—no questions asked—and then he'd seen her safely to the airport himself the following morning.

'Not Luigi's?' Vito asked, a vertical crease forming between his brows as he studied her. 'Why not?'

'It's up to you, if you're set on going there.' Lily stumbled for words. She'd done nothing wrong, but Vito was a proud Venetian man, and she knew instinctively that he would not appreciate the fact that she'd accepted help from another man. 'But I'd really love to go out to that place on Burano. I've got a craving for fish.'

'Very well.' Turning to leave, Vito suddenly stopped and pinned her with his piercing blue gaze. 'This meal is a celebration,' he said. 'Wear something suitable for such an occasion.'

Lily stared at his retreating back in irritation, wondering if he'd deliberately meant to provoke her by being so autocratic. It was hard to get used to the way he was treating her now. He'd always been a dominant force, but he'd never blatantly ordered her about before.

She stood up and walked across the room to look out of the tall, arched window. Sleek black gondolas loaded with tourists glided past on the jade-green canal below. She watched the languid ripples glimmering on the surface of the water, thinking about how her life had changed.

She wasn't a tourist any more. She wasn't even a visitor. She was in Venice to stay.

She pulled her thoughts together and headed upstairs to dress for dinner. She'd show Vito that she understood the rules of the game. He wouldn't need to waste his time approving her choice of wardrobe—her instincts for self-preservation wouldn't allow her to put herself through that humiliation again.

She'd accepted that Vito was utterly serious in his intention to marry her, and although the circumstances were not what she would have chosen she was determined to make the best of the situation.

She owed it to herself not to let the virile, masculine power of his personality completely overshadow her. She must take on the responsibility of creating a life for herself in Venice, and to prepare a place in this family for her unborn child.

And she knew that the best route forward was to stop fighting against Vito, to find a way to work within his rules. The way to stand up for herself was to be proactive. It would be better to try to influence how things happened in the first place, rather than battle with Vito after the event.

A little while later they were zipping across the lagoon towards the island of Burano.

'I've missed being out on the water,' Lily said, glancing at Vito. The golden evening light gilded his jet-black hair and cast a warm glow over his face, but his features were set in a shuttered expression. There was no way of knowing what he was thinking. 'It was one of my favourite things about living here, even though it was winter.'

'You never did seem to feel the cold,' Vito said shortly. Then, despite the fact it should have been obvious she was trying to start a conversation, he fell silent again, his expression still closed to her.

With a small sigh, Lily turned to look at the view, determined to enjoy the rest of the boat trip. The low angle of the sun across the water was creating a beautiful effect—dark indigo waves rippled against golden-orange ribbons of reflected sunlight. It was true that she'd always loved being out on the lagoon, and she wasn't going to let Vito's brooding silence mar her pleasure in the amazing view.

Before long they were approaching the picturesque island. With its gaily painted houses and simple style, it seemed a million miles away from Venice. There were no hotels on the island, and as the evening drew in the tourists disappeared back to the city. The local artisans packed away their handmade lace and other crafts, and fishermen and their families came outside to enjoy an evening stroll.

The driver brought the boat to a standstill on one side of the harbour, then jumped out athletically to tie the craft up. Vito disembarked first, turning to offer Lily support as she climbed out of the swaying boat onto the quayside.

She reached for him automatically, but the instant their hands made contact a jolt of highly charged sensual energy ran through her. She snatched her hand away with a gasp, then stumbled awkwardly as the boat lurched with the movement of the water.

Vito's fingers closed around her forearm, his grip strong and steadying, but he didn't speak as she climbed out onto the quay.

'Thank you.' She tried to make her voice bright and breezy as they started walking towards the main street, but it sounded strained to her own ears. Why should simply taking his hand make her so sexually aware of him? Out of the blue her body was humming with desire for him—even though he hadn't done or said anything much since they'd left home. 'I should know better than to make sudden movements when I'm standing on the edge of a boat.'

She lifted her eyes to his face, and the way he was looking at her suddenly made her mouth run dry. She looked away skittishly, waiting a moment for him to speak, but it seemed he was continuing to maintain a charged silence.

'For goodness' sake!' Lily stopped in her tracks and turned to stare up at him. 'Stop giving me the silent treatment. You're the one who wants us to keep up appearances.'

'What do you want me to say?' Vito asked, with an infuriating lift to one black eyebrow before he turned and continued walking towards the restaurant. 'Should I reprimand you for acting foolishly at the water's edge? Or would you like to talk about how the simple touch of my hand on yours sent shock waves of sexual desire burning through you?'

'No it didn't,' Lily said indignantly, feeling hot colour flood to her cheeks as she hurried to keep pace beside him. The very mention of sexual desire was doing things to her that she'd rather deny, especially given Vito's current rather arrogant and hostile mood. She was glad now that they were walking along and he wasn't looking at her any more.

'Of course it did. And, if something as simple as touching hands turns you on, whatever will happen at the restaurant when I take you in my arms and make a show of how happy we are together?' His voice rumbled through her, setting her nerves alight.

His absolute confidence in his effect on her bothered her on more levels than she could say. Even thinking about the fact that he could turn her on was doing exactly that. She could feel her skin start to flush, and her heart rate had definitely speeded up.

'Why can't we have a proper conversation?' Lily protested, trying to ignore the way she was feeling.

'We could try,' Vito said, as he held the door for her to walk into the restaurant. 'But you might as well face up to it—not much else is going to hold your attention. We both know how this evening has to end.'

Mental pictures of Vito making love to her whirled through her mind, and she could feel her body buzzing with anticipation. Try as she might, it was impossible to ignore the images and the way they were making her feel.

Lily's cheeks were scarlet as the *maître d'* rushed over to them, fussing about how long it had been since their last visit, and showing them to the best table in the restaurant.

'Your usual glass of prosecco to begin?' he asked.

'That would be perfect.' Vito flashed Lily a lazy smile that sent a frisson skittering through her. 'After all, this is an evening of celebration.'

'I shouldn't drink more than a few sips,' she said. For some reason she shied away from mentioning her pregnancy.

'What is it you English say?' Vito asked, with a devilish glint in his eyes. '"A little of what you fancy does you good"?'

Lily's face was glowing and she could feel herself actually trembling. She told herself it was just nerves magnifying her reaction to his provocation, and buried her head in the menu to avoid his piercing gaze.

If she was going to get through the evening unscathed, she had to get herself in check. She forced herself to read the menu, concentrating very hard on all the options, to chase all other thoughts out of her mind.

She was feeling slightly more composed when the waiter came to tell them the special fish dishes available from the day's catch, and she was pleased at the extra distraction. By the time they had both made their selections, she had more or less clamped down on her wayward reaction to Vito, although she knew her control was pretty tenuous. She'd have to work very hard to keep the conversation neutral.

'We should discuss wedding arrangements.' Vito suddenly spoke, taking her by surprise with his change of tack.

'Of course,' Lily replied, overwhelmingly relieved that he had apparently given up his campaign to make her feel uncomfortable. She picked up her prosecco glass and took a sip of the sparkling white wine that the Veneto region was famous for. The delicate bubbles fizzed pleasantly in her mouth, and for a moment she felt the tension start to drain out of her body.

'It must be very soon,' Vito continued. 'And I think a relatively small family affair would be best. Is there anyone you wish to invite who would be able to come at short notice?'

'I don't know. I hadn't really thought.' Lily smoothed her hand over her long hair in sudden consternation. It was going to be strange enough going through with the wedding. And nothing had changed regarding her concerns about keeping up appearances with her mother or best friends being there. 'You know, I think it would be better to tell them afterwards. Maybe they can visit later.'

'Ashamed of your fiancé?' Vito asked. His tone was utterly neutral, and for a disconcerting moment Lily wondered if he was offended or being sardonic.

'No.' She looked him squarely in the eye. A couple of months ago she would have been so proud to call him that. 'I'm just not sure I'll be able to convince the people I love that this is real. I'm still getting used to it.'

'All right,' he said. 'If you think it would be best, we'll keep it very small. Just my grandfather—if he's well enough—and a couple of witnesses.'

He continued to hold her gaze for a long moment, his blue eyes looking smoky in the candlelight, and for a second Lily had a flash of how it used to be between them. She was glad he had accepted what she said without making more of it. She knew she had to make the marriage look normal—and she had very good reasons for going ahead with it. But it was still too soon to be confident that she'd manage in front of the people who loved and knew her best.

The rest of the meal passed smoothly. Vito kept the conversation light, for which she was very grateful, and by the time Lily had finished her ice cream she was surprised to realise that she had actually enjoyed a proper meal for the first time in weeks. Maybe her body was finally settling into the second trimester of her pregnancy and the misery of morning sickness was over.

'Let's go home,' Vito said, signalling for the bill.

Lily looked at him, suddenly remembering what he had said about them both knowing how the evening would end. A dark shiver of anticipation ran through her. She couldn't deny that she missed the nights of passion they had shared.

Her skin was flushing again, and she stared at the paintings covering the walls to take her mind off making love with Vito. On their earlier visits to the restaurant he had told her how previous owners had sometimes accepted paintings as payment for meals. As a result the walls were covered with an astonishingly eclectic array of artwork that she'd always enjoyed looking at—but right then it wasn't enough to distract her from the thought of lying in Vito's arms.

It was dark as they travelled back across the lagoon, and a beautiful crescent moon hung in the sky. Lily shivered, hugging her silk wrap tighter around her—not because she was cold, but because of the way Vito had started looking at her again.

It was too dark to see his features clearly, but she could sense his expression was the one she had seen so many times before when they'd been lovers. The expression that meant very soon they would be making love.

'You're cold,' Vito said, slipping his arm around her shoulder and pulling her closer to his side.

'Not really,' Lily responded, leaning against his hard muscled body with a ripple of pleasure. Half a glass of prosecco had gone to her head—or maybe she was simply intoxicated by her proximity to Vito. His spicy masculine aroma was filling her senses, making her body sing with remembered sensations.

'You're trembling,' Vito murmured, leaning close to her ear. She could feel his lips moving deliciously against her hair. Excitement knotted deep inside her, making her shiver in expectation of what was to happen later.

'I'm not really cold.' The words came out in a small, shaky voice, and she realised that although she yearned to lie in his arms again she was also extremely nervous. Would it be as good as she remembered? Would Vito be satisfied with her?

Their physical compatibility was the one thing that might create a genuine bond between them in their marriage of convenience. Or was she placing too much significance on it? Would it ever again be more than just sex to Vito?

'I've missed this, *bella mia*.' Vito's deep, sensual

voice rumbled right through her as he lifted his hands to turn her face towards him. His fingers slipped between the silky tresses of her hair, and he inclined her head slightly to one side, as if he was about to kiss her.

Lily gazed at him silently. Her heart was racing and she wanted to feel his lips against hers, experience the mastery of his kiss again. But for a long moment he didn't move.

'So have I,' she whispered, thinking about the time when it had been natural for her to pull him close for a kiss. Before she thought about what she was doing, she leant nearer and pressed a light kiss against his mouth.

For a heartbeat she held her breath. He hadn't kissed her back. Maybe this wasn't the way he wanted it to be now. But her lips tingled with the feel of his firm, sensual mouth and she was desperate for him to kiss her properly.

Suddenly Vito began to move and everything seemed to happen at once. His strong hands were under the hem of her full skirt, sliding rapidly up the outside of her legs, making the breath catch in her throat. Then, before she realised what he was doing, he took hold of her hips and lifted her so that she was sitting astride him.

She grabbed hold of his broad shoulders to steady herself as desire flooded through her, pooling at the very centre of her womanhood. Her most sensitive feminine place was now pressed intimately against him. She could feel his erection pushing powerfully against her through his trousers. They were in a perfect position for making love—and sensation stormed through her quivering body, as if that was really what they were doing.

The movement of the boat as it bounced lightly over the waves bumped their bodies together erotically, and Lily felt her breath coming in shorter and shorter gasps. In a distant, rational part of her mind, she couldn't believe how aroused she was. He'd barely touched her and he hadn't even kissed her. Yet her body was on fire.

His hands were still under her skirt, resting on her hips and pulling her into close contact with him. She longed to feel those hands glide across her, but for a moment they stayed perfectly still.

'I want to touch you all over,' he murmured as his hands started to move.

Her knees on the seat were supporting her, and there was room for him to slide his hands around the curve of her bottom. She bit the tip of her tongue lightly between her teeth. His fingers left a tingling trail in their wake—but she needed more.

'Kiss me.' His words were a command, but suddenly she wondered if he was playing a game with her. A moment ago he hadn't kissed her back. Would he respond this time? Or would he sit there as cold as stone—despite the fact he knew how turned on she was, and that she could feel how hard he was?

Her position astride him meant that her head was slightly higher than his. She leant forward and brushed her lips lightly over his. He was driving her wild with frustrated sexual need—she'd try to give him a taste of his own medicine.

But as soon as their lips made contact another rush of overwhelming desire stormed her body and, almost as if from a distance, she heard a low, sexy moan emerge from deep within her.

Suddenly Vito lifted his hand and cupped the nape of her neck. He pulled her mouth down roughly to his, and kissed her with a furious passion that matched the pent-up energy burning inside her. His tongue plunged in deeply and she took it willingly, inviting the rough, sensual invasion of her mouth. She wanted to taste him, feel him. She wanted to be as close to him as possible.

They'd never kissed like this before. All through the many wild or tender nights they'd shared, she had never experienced a kiss so intense. The blood was singing in her ears, blotting out everything but Vito and her over-powering need to be with him.

Then she felt his other hand push up between them, pulling at the buttons on the front of her dress. A moment later his hand was inside, slipping under the lace of her bra to cup her breast. A deep sigh of plea-sure escaped her, but he kept on kissing, delving deeper with his tongue as his fingers found her nipple and teased it.

Sensation spiralled out from her breast and she finally pulled back from his kiss, gasping for air.

'Oh, Vito.' She breathed deeply, feeling her body shuddering against him.

'You're ready for me.' One hand was still inside her bra, doing exquisite things to her breast, and he slipped the other under the curtain of hair that had fallen forward over them. He pushed it behind her shoulder, then pulled her silk wrap closely around her to cover the open front of her dress. 'And as soon as we are inside I'm going to make you mine, once and for all.'

His words of possession rolled through her body like an incredible promise. She wanted to be his. She'd always been his. From the moment that they'd met he had been the master of her body, able to lift her to heights she had never imagined possible. Able to make her world splinter into a million points of absolute bliss, where nothing mattered but being with Vito.

She made a murmur of protest as he slipped his hand gently from her dress, then she realised that the boat had already slowed down as it wound its way through the canals of the city. In a minute they would be at the *palazzo*.

The boat glided up to the gothic arch of the water gate, and Vito lifted her from his lap. Her legs were unsteady, and before she realised what he was doing he pulled her wrap tightly around her and swept her up into his arms. A lifetime of watercraft and canals had made him nimble on his feet, and within a moment he had whisked her off the boat and carried her straight up to their bedroom.

CHAPTER SEVEN

HE LAID her on the bed and stood over her, discarding his jacket and tie, before kneeling beside her and finishing off undoing the buttons on her dress.

She gazed up at him, smiling at the way his fringe had fallen forward over his face. She reached up to run her fingers through his luxuriant black hair, while he unbuttoned her dress.

Touching his hair suddenly seemed a curiously intimate thing to do. It was silly to think that, considering what had happened on the boat and what was about to happen. But for that moment she found herself thinking that everything would be all right. She could almost imagine the past six weeks had never happened.

'I've missed this,' Vito said, slipping her dress off her shoulders and pulling it all the way down under her hips.

He let his gaze wander over her as she lay on the bed dressed in nothing but a lacy bra, French knickers, hold-up stockings and high-heeled shoes.

She was gorgeous.

'You are beautiful,' he murmured, cupping one breast in each hand. They were deliciously warm beneath his fingers, and he felt her nipples harden instantly against his palms.

She was moving restlessly on the bed, and he knew it wouldn't take much to bring her back to a state of heightened arousal. She had been unbelievably responsive to him out on the lagoon, and knowing how he was affecting her had also been a powerful aphrodisiac for him. Not that she'd ever had to do much to turn him on—he'd been hot for her from the moment he'd first laid eyes on her. And tonight he planned to lay more on her than just his eyes. They were to be married, and he would make her his wife in every sense.

With skilful fingers he slipped his hands behind her back to unhook her bra, and as he tossed it to one side he saw her start to tremble again. Her pupils were dilated with her building need, and as she arched her back, thrusting her breasts up towards him, he knew exactly what she wanted.

'Oh!' Lily cried out as his mouth closed over her nipple. Glorious feelings rippled through her body, as his sinuous tongue worked magic on her tingling flesh. 'Oh, Vito!' She said his name again. She couldn't believe she was really here, that this was really happening. Vito was making love to her again, and everything would be as it had been.

His hands were moving over her body, burning a trail wherever they touched, removing her French knickers and stockings, urging her pulse rate up and up.

She lay naked on the bed, breathing raggedly as Vito finally lifted his head to look at her. A knot of sexual excitement twisted inside her as she gazed into his darkened eyes. She knew he wanted her as much as her body was aching for him.

But he was wearing too many clothes. She needed to feel his skin against hers, run her hands over his hard, muscled body. She reached up to undo his shirt.

'This is good.' Vito's voice was husky as he looked

down at her fingers struggling with his buttons. 'I should have remembered—eating out always made you amorous.'

'No, it didn't,' Lily protested, finally tossing his shirt away. Then she paused and stared at him, suddenly thinking back to when they'd lived together. Some of their most romantic evenings *had* involved an evening out.

'Ah—now you remember,' Vito drawled, lazily pulling his black leather belt through the loop on his trousers.

'It wasn't eating out,' Lily replied.

A strangely hollow feeling moved through her as she suddenly realised that it had been more about having his attention. When he'd spent an evening with her—rather than working—it had made her feel special. Wanted. Worthy of him.

When he'd slipped into bed beside her after a night spent in his office she'd always welcomed him into her arms. But it hadn't been the same. She'd taken pleasure from knowing that he sought comfort in her arms after a long day of work. But it was never the same as when he'd spent time with her.

'We'll test it again tomorrow,' Vito said, his voice tickling her stomach as he leant forward and scattered kisses over her sensitive skin. 'We'll go to Luigi's.'

Without meaning to, Lily felt herself tense.

Vito sat up and looked at her sharply.

'What is it?' he demanded, his voice cold and hard. 'When I mentioned Luigi earlier you acted strangely. Tell me what this is about.'

'Nothing,' Lily said, pushing herself up onto her elbows and suddenly feeling acutely conscious of the fact that she was naked.

'Tell me.' Vito swore and lurched angrily to his feet. 'Is *he* the one? Is he the one you betrayed me with?'

'No!' Lily gasped. She hugged her knees up to her chest and looked at him in alarm. A terrifying change had come over him, darkening his features and making the room crackle with angry energy.

'I'll ask him!' He snatched up his shirt and started to pull it on jerkily.

'No!' Lily cried in horror. She couldn't let Vito storm out to confront Luigi. He'd been her guardian angel that night—she couldn't bear him to suffer Vito's rage because of his kindness. 'Listen. It's not what you think—I'll tell you what happened.'

'Speak quickly,' Vito said, reaching for his jacket. 'Then, when I've heard your lies, I'll go and hear what Luigi has to say.'

'He'll tell you how he found me alone, with nowhere to go, on the night you threw me out!' She stared up at him, painful memories bombarding her.

'Continue,' Vito grated, his face dark with barely contained fury.

'The fog closed the airport.' She took a breath, but she knew her voice was still shaky. 'It was a few days before Easter—everywhere was fully booked. I couldn't find a hotel—'

'Are you trying to tell me every hotel room in Venice was full?' Vito demanded. 'Don't be absurd.'

'It was already late when I left here,' she said, re-membering how sick and miserable she'd felt, dragging herself from hotel to hotel. 'I'd stopped for a moment, down the alley near Luigi's, trying to think what to do. He saw me standing there, alone with my luggage.'

'Go on.' Vito's frown was thunderous, creating a deep vertical crease between his brows and casting his eyes into dark shadow.

'He was very kind. He took me to his mother's

house, because she has a spare room,' Lily said quietly. 'That's all.'

She looked up at him, anxious that he should believe her—as much for Luigi's sake as her own. But he remained ominously silent.

Suddenly she found herself wondering how Vito felt. Did he care at all that she had been alone and unprotected that night in Venice, with no one to turn to and nowhere to seek refuge? She hugged her knees tighter, pressing her forehead against them and letting her hair fall forwards in a curtain around her.

He didn't care. He'd never really cared about her. A passing acquaintance had cared more for her well-being that night than Vito.

Humiliation gnawed at her. What was she doing here? Why was she here with a man who didn't care about her and didn't even have the slightest respect for her?

'Don't hide from me.'

Vito's voice cut through her misery like cold steel. She lifted her head in time to see him reaching for her—then suddenly she was standing beside the bed facing him.

'I wasn't hiding.' She tossed her hair back over her shoulders defiantly, despite the fact it bared her breasts to him again. She was completely naked, while he was almost completely dressed. But she refused to let herself think about that.

'We will never discuss the night you left Venice again,' Vito said. 'Tomorrow we eat at Luigi's—showing everyone that we are an ecstatic couple about to be married.'

'As you wish,' Lily responded stiffly, thinking that Luigi was bound to be curious as to what had happened.

'It is unacceptable that you turned to Luigi,' Vito continued, his voice throbbing with intensity. 'Mark my words—you will *never* again take our problems outside of this bedroom. Whatever happens,' he grated, 'our affairs are private.'

'You threw me out!' Lily cried in her defence.

'But now you're back.' Vito's eyes swept over her, leaving a trail of sexual awareness prickling over her naked body. 'And you must take the consequences of your actions.'

'What is that supposed to mean?' Lily stood tall, resisting the urge to fidget under his hot eyes.

'That you are mine.' His voice was loaded with sexual possessiveness. 'And you will do anything I want.'

'I've always done whatever you want,' Lily threw back at him.

It was true, she realised to her shame. Except when they'd been together it had always seemed that they wanted the same thing.

'Not always,' Vito growled, seizing her roughly and dragging her up against him. He loomed over her, plunging his hands into her hair and pulling her head back so that their faces were only inches apart. 'But now you're mine—*only mine*. No other man is ever going to touch you again.'

He dragged her closer, bumping their hips together erotically. Lily gasped at the intimate contact just as his lips closed, hot and demanding, over hers.

His tongue pushed into her mouth, stoking the sexual fire that was suddenly raging between them once more. Desire for him rushed through her veins, making her insides tingle and her legs turn to water.

A pulsing point of sensation starting throbbing between her legs, and the feel of his hands running over her naked skin was driving her wild with her own need to touch him.

He pulled away from her abruptly, and shrugged his jacket off. Lily stood shakily, taking shallow breaths as she watched him discarding his clothes. Her gaze drifted up to his face.

What she saw made her heart miss a beat.

He was furious.

She could see the anger burning in his eyes, pulling the muscles in his face taut with tension. He was still absolutely livid about her supposed infidelity, and this was an act of vengeance.

'No.' Lily took a step backwards.

'You can't back out now.' Vito moved towards her, and lifted his hand to cup her breast. His thumb toyed with her nipple, and an answering ripple of delight spread through her body. 'You are mine to take, whenever I choose.'

'You're not going to make love to me out of anger,' Lily said, trying to ignore the feel of his hand on her breast and the sensual pleasure his touch was giving her.

'I'm taking back what is mine.'

'I was always yours.' Lily's voice was small and steady, despite the turmoil of emotions and physical sensations that was assailing her.

Almost before her words were finished, he moved forwards and pulled her into his arms again. His mouth came down to kiss her, and as his tongue thrust between her lips it was as if he was staking his claim in the most basic way.

Her treacherous body was responding to his. Despite her mind protesting that this was not right—that she had to stop him if she was to maintain any self-respect—her flesh was aching with her need for him. Deep inside she was vibrating with her desire to feel him lying on top of her, thrusting into her. Making her his again.

Suddenly he pulled away.

His breathing was ragged as he stood looking at her for a moment, his expression utterly impenetrable. Then he turned on his heel and walked out.

Lily stared after him—beset by conflicting emotions.

It was what she'd wanted, wasn't it?

Then why did she feel so bereft?

Lily stood by the window, looking down at the canal below, wondering how she could make things better between Vito and herself. It was several weeks since they'd been married, and she was still having trouble adjusting to it.

It was hard to believe it was actually real, especially as Vito had hardly come near her since the night he had stormed out of the bedroom. At first she'd assumed he was simply cooling off—she'd known how angry he was. But then the wedding had come and gone, with only the bare formalities discussed between them.

It had been a small, private ceremony, and the simple occasion had scarcely caused a blip in the passage of time. It was extraordinary that such a momentous life event had slipped past without greater impact. But then it had not been a normal wedding. And as the weeks had continued to pass it was painfully clear that it was not a normal marriage.

She almost felt like she was stuck in a time warp—with nothing really changing and every day the same. Vito had continued to share the bedroom, but he worked late most nights, often coming to bed after midnight. And, although weeks had passed, he'd never touched her.

She knew he was worried about his grandfather. His instinct that his grandfather's health was not right on Lily's first day back in Venice had proved to be correct, because Giovanni had soon gone down with a nasty chest-infection. But, from the little information Lily was able to glean, that appeared to have cleared up now.

She turned away from the window, planning to sit and read for a while before going out for a walk, when a movement from the doorway caught her eye.

'Vito.' She said his name in surprise. It was barely ten o'clock in the morning—he never came home from work during the day. 'Is everything all right? Your grandfather...?'

'Yes,' Vito replied. 'In fact that is why I am here. My grandfather's health is much improved. This morning would be a suitable time for you to meet him.'

'I'll go and get my bag.' Lily walked towards the door, then hesitated as Vito didn't step aside to let her through. She held her breath and slipped past him, feeling the hairs on her arms stand up and her heart-rate increase, as she couldn't help brushing lightly against him.

She tried to ignore the feeling as she ran up the stairs to the bedroom. She paused in front of the mirror to check her appearance, and was disconcerted to see her flushed cheeks and animated eyes.

Was it the simple contact of brushing against him that had caused the light in her face? Or was it the prospect of spending a little time in Vito's company?

Whatever the case, she didn't ponder it, and as she didn't need to change her clothes she hurried back down the stairs. Ever since the first morning in Venice she had taken trouble with her appearance. She didn't want to give Vito another opportunity to humiliate her.

The walk to *Ca' Salvatore* didn't take long, and as they arrived at the baroque *palazzo* Vito took her hand in his. A charge of energy passed between them and, as Lily felt herself tremble, she realised it was the first proper physical contact they'd shared since the night they'd nearly made love.

Vito had not touched her since then, and the fact that he had chosen this moment to hold her hand made it clear to Lily that his intention was to show all at *Ca' Salvatore* that she was his. It was a reminder of how important it was to Vito that his grandfather saw them as a proper couple.

He led her into the beautiful building and up to the second-floor room where Giovanni was resting in bed.

'*Nonno*, there is someone I'd like you to meet,' Vito said. He crossed the room to kiss his grandfather's cheek. Then, putting his arm round the old man's shoulders, he helped him up into a sitting position.

'We're speaking in English?' Giovanni asked, squinting across the room short-sightedly. 'Very intriguing. I'd better put my spectacles on.'

Lily smiled. Despite her nervousness, she was already warming to the old man. His body might be frail, but his mind was certainly active.

'They're here, with your newspaper.' She slipped around to the other side of the large bed and handed his spectacles to him.

'Thank you, my dear. No, stay close,' Giovanni added, his bony hand shooting out to catch her arm and pull her closer. 'So I can get a proper look at you.'

'*Nonno!*' Vito chided gently. 'Let go of Lily, and I'll introduce you properly.'

'Formalities!' Giovanni scoffed, although he did release his grip. 'What use are formalities at my age? Tell me quickly—who is this beautiful young English woman? And why have you brought her to meet me?'

'This is Lily,' Vito said. 'And I'm very pleased to tell you that—'

'Yes, yes—get on with it,' Giovanni urged.

'That she is my wife,' Vito finished smoothly, not at all phased by his grandfather's interruption.

'Your wife?' Giovanni said. 'Why didn't I know about this?'

'You were sick, *Nonno*,' Vito said. 'I thought it best to go ahead with the wedding and tell you when you were feeling better.'

'You were married without me?' Giovanni said, sounding slightly affronted as he looked sharply at Vito, then across at Lily. 'So you've finally come to your senses and decided to settle down?'

'Yes, *Nonno*,' Vito said, hugging Lily in an open display of affection. She leant into his embrace, taking comfort from the feel of his strong arms around her, despite the knowledge that it was only for show. A whirl of conflicting thoughts and emotions was flowing through her, but she fought to keep a clear head and pay attention to the exchange between Vito and his grand-father. 'It was a very small wedding,' Vito added.

Just how significant had Giovanni's desire to see his grandson settled been in Vito's sudden proposal? Every-thing had happened so quickly at first, and in the interven-ing time she still hadn't come any closer to figuring out Vito's motivation. She had married him for her child's sake—but she didn't really understand what was in it for Vito. Especially as he seemed to be avoiding her.

'So you found the right woman after all?' Giovanni probed, leaning forward and peering closely at Lily. 'An English rose—or should I say an English lily? The name is certainly appropriate.'

'The right woman,' Vito repeated, placing a brief kiss on Lily's cheek. '*Si, Nonno*. You always told me that in time I would find the right woman.'

The old man snorted, wicked humour making his eyes brighten. 'I said that, did I? I seem to remember talking to you just a few days before I got that wretched infection,' he said. 'I told you to hurry up and provide me with an heir. Is that what this is?'

Lily barely managed to shield her shocked reaction. Her heart jerked painfully in her chest, and for a second she struggled to draw air into her lungs. Then she became aware of Vito beside her.

He had gone utterly rigid. A horrible sensation cut through her. It was as if she could actually feel his pain as his muscles tensed with agonising intensity.

'You went on a business trip to London,' Giovanni said. 'What did you do—propose to the first attractive girl you met?'

'No, *Nonno*. That's not how it happened…' Vito looked at his grandfather's face and suddenly ran out of words.

This wasn't how it had been supposed to go. The wily old man had completely wrong-footed him— and if he didn't pull himself together quickly it would all be for nothing. If he couldn't convince his grandfather that his relationship with Lily was genuine, he might not accept her child as his heir. It wouldn't make him content.

And that was what this was all about—fulfilling Giovanni's dying wish to see his name continued. What kind of grandson was he if he couldn't do the one thing that would make his beloved grandfather happy in his dying days? After everything his grandfather had done for him, this was the one thing that any man ought to be able to do in return.

His shame at his failure bore into him, burning a hole in his chest, making it hard to think, impossible to speak.

'It's true we arrived from London the day before you

got sick,' Lily suddenly spoke up, her voice quiet but clear in the high-ceilinged chamber. 'But we didn't just meet.'

'Tell me more.' Giovanni leant forward, as if it would help him catch everything she said.

'We first met nearly a year ago,' Lily said, stepping closer to the bed. 'After several months of travelling between London and Venice for weekends and holidays, Vito asked me to move in with him here. I've been living in Venice with him since Novem…'

Vito looked at her sharply as her words petered out. He'd been amazed, and very relieved, that she'd spoken up. But now she was blushing and looking down at the floor, letting her blonde hair swing forward to conceal her face.

'What is it?' Giovanni barked. 'Why did you stop talking?'

'I…it just occurred to me that you might be Catholic.' Lily looked up and continued hesitantly. 'That you might not approve of us living together. I'm sorry— that's probably why Vito never brought me here before.'

Giovanni's bark of laughter broke the sudden tension in the room.

'Now I see.' The old man spoke between chuckles. 'You were taking your time, making sure it was right. After Capricia, I can understand your caution.'

'It seemed wise to be sure,' Vito said, turning to look at Lily. He didn't know why she had said what she'd said—whether she was defending him, or simply acting out the role she had agreed to. Or maybe she was just naively speaking her mind.

Whatever the explanation, relief flooded through him, and he hugged her to him in an embrace that was entirely natural. Her guileless chatter had utterly won over his grandfather, and for that he was thankful.

Suddenly he found himself thinking how different Lily was from his ex-wife Capricia. In fact, she was different from all the other women he had ever been involved with.

Capricia's heart was as hard and impenetrable as a diamond. Her scornful face flashed unpleasantly through his mind, and he knew he could never have employed the same tactics of persuasion on her that he had used on Lily.

For some reason the thought made him uncomfortable, but he pushed it ruthlessly to the back of his mind. Just because Lily had her weaknesses did not mean she didn't deserve everything she got. He couldn't forget she had betrayed him by sleeping with another man.

'But now something has changed.' Vito turned back to his grandfather and continued speaking. 'Something that has made us look to the future.'

'What's that?' Giovanni sat up straighter, and from the sharp expression on his face Vito thought he had guessed what was coming next.

'Lily is pregnant,' he said. 'You are the first one to share our wonderful news.'

For a moment Giovanni looked stunned. It was as if the news, which he'd waited so many years to hear, was suddenly too much to take in. Then a massive smile spread across his old face.

Lily watched as his eyes started to sparkle with unshed tears and, even though she had only just met Vito's grandfather, she understood how important this was to him. Impulsively, she leant over the bed and kissed his cheek.

'You've made me very happy,' he said. 'My name will continue. There will be Salvatores living at *Ca' Salvatore.*'

Lily smiled at him, thinking how different life was

for Vito's family. After her upbringing, it was hard to imagine living in a palace that had been in the family for hundreds of years.

'What do you think of Venice?' Giovanni suddenly asked. 'People say it's old and crumbling—like me.' There was a merry twinkle in his eyes that made him look years younger, but Lily knew that the question was important to him. 'But I say there's life in the old dog yet. What do you think, Lily?'

'Oh, definitely.' Lily smiled warmly and leant forward to take his hand. She could feel a slight tremor, and despite the fact she had only just met him she knew that he was tiring. 'It couldn't be more different from the green and open countryside where I grew up—but I absolutely love it. It's beautiful, fascinating, and there is always more to see.'

'Not too crowded for you?' he pressed. 'After the quiet of the countryside?'

'I love the hustle and bustle,' Lily said truthfully. 'And if I want some space around me I can walk beside the water, or take a boat out onto the lagoon.'

Giovanni leant back against his pillows. His body looked frail, but there was a light in his faded blue eyes.

'You're tired, *Nonno*,' Vito said. 'We should leave you to rest.'

'No, wait a moment,' Giovanni suddenly said. 'Look in the top drawer—a wooden box.'

'Is this what you mean?' Vito asked, holding up a highly polished, flat wooden box that he'd found in the old chest-of-drawers across the room.

'Give it to Lily,' Giovanni said.

Vito frowned, but did as his grandfather bid. Lily took the box hesitantly, caught between the displeasure on Vito's face and Giovanni's wishes.

'Oh!' she gasped as she opened the box to reveal a stunningly beautiful necklace. 'It's exquisite!'

'Antique Venetian glass,' Giovanni said. 'It was *my* great-grandmother's. Until now I didn't have anyone to pass it on to. It's for you, my dear. Welcome to my family.'

Lily stared at the antique jewellery in awe. She'd never seen anything so gorgeous—and knowing that the glass beads were hundreds of years old, that the necklace had been treasured for generations, made it even more special.

'We can't accept that, *Nonno*,' Vito said.

'I'm not giving it to *you*.' Giovanni looked sternly at his grandson, then his watery gaze moved on to Lily. 'Your wife appreciates it. From her expression, I can see that she knows the true value of the necklace.'

'Vito's right,' Lily said, reluctantly closing the lid of the box. 'This is too much. You've only just met me.'

'That doesn't matter. You are my granddaughter now,' Giovanni said. He leant back against his plump pillows and closed his eyes. 'You may leave now. I am tired.'

Lily clutched the box tightly as Vito steered her out of the *palazzo*. It had been a morning full of surprises.

They walked home quietly. Lily had a lot on her mind. There were still so many questions—but at least some things were starting to come clear. Vito's grandfather was a wonderful old man, and she understood completely why Vito wanted to make his last days happy. But he wasn't being honest with anyone.

It wasn't long before they were back in their bedroom.

'I wish you had told me.' Lily spoke without preamble. 'That the only reason you wanted to marry me is to make your grandfather's final days happier.'

'There was no need to complicate our arrangement.' Vito spoke shortly, not bothering to deny her accusation. 'It was not your concern.'

'Of course it was,' Lily said. 'I'm involved! I'm the one carrying your child—Giovanni's great-grandchild. And I'm the one who is going to spend time with him during his last months.'

'Save that for the rest of the world,' Vito snapped. 'Endless repetition won't make it true, so stop trying to convince me that the child is mine.'

'But it *is*,' Lily protested. 'Whatever you say, *I'm* not going to stop believing it—or saying it—because it is true.'

'My grandfather is old and frail. He doesn't have long to live.' Vito brutally brought the subject back around. 'It is the *thought* that his family line will continue that he needs. Not to socialise with you.'

Lily stared at him bitterly. Despite the circumstances, she had enjoyed meeting Giovanni. He was a wonderful old man, and she was sure spending time with him would enrich her life.

'Oh my God!' she gasped suddenly, sitting down on the edge of the bed as her legs felt weak with shock. 'As far as you're concerned, this is a temporary arrangement. As soon as Giovanni passes away, you're planning to throw me and the baby out again!'

She looked up at Vito in a silent appeal, desperate for him to tell her that she was wrong. But he just stared down at her, a hard, unfeeling expression on his face.

'Your grandfather will have died happy.' At last Lily spoke her awful train of thought aloud. 'And you will have no further use for me. Or for the baby. No wonder you were able to suggest this, even though you are adamant that the baby isn't yours!'

'It was a practical solution,' Vito said coldly. 'And now you'll finally understand that it is pointless for you to continually try to persuade me of your innocence. Or to build a relationship with my grandfather. Or to put down roots in Venice. As soon as his time comes, you'll be history.'

Lily stared at him in horror as the cold brutality of his words sunk in.

'You are a despicable human being!' she cried, suddenly flying to her feet and squaring up to him. 'You don't deserve a grandfather who loves you so much!'

'I didn't deserve a lover who cheated on me.' The angry blue fire sparking in his eyes was the only sign of emotion on his face.

Lily glared at him, struggling for words. She couldn't believe Vito would really do something like this.

All the time she'd lived with him she'd thought him to be a fair and generous man. That had changed the day he'd thrown her out for getting pregnant. Then, when he'd asked her to marry him, she'd been forced to rethink her opinion for a second time.

She knew he was angry and upset because he believed she had betrayed him but after this latest, awful revelation her opinion of him had sunk to the lowest depths—into a confusing emotional mass of disbelief and disillusionment.

'Give that to me,' Vito said, lifting the antique-necklace box from her hands. 'You can't wear that.'

Lily stared at the box as he carried it away, her temper suddenly sparking again.

'No wonder you didn't want Giovanni to give it to me,' she said bitterly. 'Don't worry. I'm not going to steal a priceless family heirloom from you.'

'It's very old and fragile,' Vito said curtly. 'The high humidity in Venice makes things deteriorate quickly. It needs expert attention to ensure it won't fall apart when you wear it.'

'I won't be wearing it,' Lily said. 'It was a wonderful gift—but you've tainted it.'

She looked up at Vito, and she could see his shoulders were rigid with tension, and a muscle was throbbing insistently on his angular jawbone. Although his eyes were cast into shadow by black brows that were drawn heavily downwards, she could see that powerful emotion glittered within them.

Perhaps he wasn't as cold and unmoved by this discussion as he would like her to think, but that didn't change his intentions.

'Once and for all, it's time to make things crystal clear between us.' His voice cut through her shattered nerves like steel wire. 'Nothing you have discovered today makes any difference to our arrangement. You did very well with my grandfather this morning—and now you will continue to play your part as my adoring wife. Until I am finished with you.'

Lily glared at him angrily, unable to find words to express the horror she was feeling.

Was he really saying that she must put up with whatever unjust accusations and hostility he chose to throw her way? That she wasn't allowed to speak up in her own defence, or express her opinion about anything?

And then, when he was done with her, that he would toss her out as callously as he'd done before—except this time she'd have a baby with her?

'You lied to me,' Lily said. 'You lied to me about making a future for our baby.'

'You lied to me first,' Vito fired back at her. 'When you tried to pass that baby off as mine.'

'You really don't care at all,' Lily said hollowly. 'You said it would be better for my baby. But how can this be better? You deceived me and manipulated me into marrying you—when all the time you were planning to dump us like last week's trash.'

'I'm not lying now,' Vito said. 'And I will not go over this again. I have made the situation plain, and I will not tolerate your defiance, or your continued assertions that I am the father of your baby.'

With that he turned and walked out of the bedroom, taking the necklace with him.

CHAPTER EIGHT

LILY stared after him in stunned silence.

All she could think was how foolish she'd been to trust Vito. She'd seen his true nature the night he'd heartlessly thrown her out onto the streets of Venice. Why, even after he'd treated her so appallingly, had she let him drag her back into his life?

Because she had once thought she was falling in love with him. And then he had lied to her. And manipulated her. He'd made her believe it was the best thing for her and her baby, when all along he couldn't have cared less about them. All he cared about was taking revenge against her for something she'd never even done. And at the same time finding a way to please his grandfather.

Lily exhaled heavily, put her hands on her hips and shook her head decisively. She wouldn't stand for it. He couldn't keep her here against her wishes. She'd leave him. Take her life back. Ruin his plans.

She grabbed her suitcase out of the wardrobe and started throwing clothes into it. Everything—all the designer clothes, the jewellery. Everything he'd ever bought her. He'd told her they were hers, and this time she'd take the lot.

Suddenly she stopped. She didn't want things he'd

paid for. She'd never cared about his money. She'd only ever cared about him. And now about her baby.

If she left, her baby would get nothing. But it wasn't about money. It was about recognition.

Her own childhood had been blighted by her father's complete refusal to have anything to do with her. It had hurt her so deeply that she'd even married a man who didn't love her to spare her baby that same heartache. Staying with Vito was the best way for her to try to get through to him. He was her baby's father—and there must be some way she could prove it to him.

'Good bye, Mum.' Lily leant forward to kiss her mother's cheek as they reached the front of the queue to go through security at Marco Polo Airport.

'Passport…boarding pass…' Ellen double-checked she was holding the crucial documents, then turned to give Lily a final hug. 'Congratulations again, darling. And thank you for having me.'

'You're welcome.' Lily smiled as warmly as she could and returned her hug.

'Oh, I'd better go!' Ellen gasped, realising she was holding up the queue. She clutched the roll of Venetian marbled paper that she hadn't wanted to crush in her suitcase and grabbed the handle of her wheelie carry-on bag.

'Thanks for coming!' Lily called.

As she stood watching her mother disappear into the departure lounge, an unpleasant feeling of emptiness crept over her. She loved her mum, but under the circumstances Ellen's visit to Venice had been tough on Lily.

Living with Vito after she had discovered the truth about his plans had been difficult. And her mother's presence hadn't made it any easier.

After their horrible row, when he'd admitted he considered their marriage temporary, things had slipped back into their previous routine disconcertingly fast. Vito had kept his distance, and Lily had not wanted to rock the boat. She instinctively knew that it would be better for her to bide her time. Starting fresh arguments with Vito was not the way to prove her innocence to him, so that he would eventually accept that he was the father of her baby.

In the end Lily had invited her mother for a few days, knowing that it was a hurdle she still had to get over. It had turned out easier than expected to convince Ellen that everything was as it should be. But, although she should have been relieved, the fact that her mother had accepted her situation so readily bothered her.

They'd never been particularly close. Ellen was nervous and highly strung—difficult to really get to know properly. When she was a child Lily had been upset by the time and effort her mother had always put into her craft projects with the patients at the hospice—while she'd forgotten to attend school events or even to buy groceries for dinner.

As she grew up Lily had told herself it was just the way her mother coped. She was disappointed with her life, and felt vulnerable being in a position of dependence on a man who was ashamed of her and wanted to keep her existence a secret.

But now Lily was feeling vulnerable. Although she knew she could not confide in Ellen, the fact that her own mother had had no inkling that anything was wrong hurt her feelings.

At first she'd mentally made excuses for her. Having stayed firmly in the countryside for years, it was natural that Ellen had been overcome by Venice. She'd wanted to spend the whole time doing touristy things. In particular she'd been fascinated by the traditional Venetian masks that were on sale all over the place.

She'd talked non-stop about new ideas for her crafting projects, and it hadn't been hard for Lily to remain virtually unnoticed. There'd been no need for her to fend off questions about why she'd married so suddenly, or about why Vito was never around. Despite the fact that it was *her* life that had suddenly changed so dramatically—and *she* was the one her mother had come to visit—she'd started to feel like the invisible woman.

She sighed as her mother disappeared into the airport departure-lounge. She couldn't help being pleased she was gone. Quite honestly, having her mother around had made her feel more alone than ever.

She turned and headed across the concourse to follow the path back down to the water, where Vito's boat was waiting for her. It was June, and a plane full of Swiss tourists had just arrived at the airport. They were all pulling their cases down the same walkway to get a water bus or taxi, but with no luggage to hold her up Lily weaved her way quickly through them. She wasn't anxious to be back at the *palazzo*, but she'd promised she'd visit Giovanni before lunch.

Vito cut the connection to his assistant and slipped his mobile phone back into his pocket.

He was pleased to have confirmation that Ellen had left Venice, but he was bothered by the news that Lily had gone straight from the airport to *Ca' Salvatore*.

Before her mother's visit Lily had started going to see his grandfather every day, and now that her mother was gone it seemed that she was getting straight back into the same pattern. Giovanni enjoyed her visits, so Vito had not put a stop to them. But it concerned him, not knowing what game Lily was playing.

After their argument he had half expected her to try to leave him. But if anything she seemed to settle into her life in Venice with more determination. He didn't know what she thought she'd gain by making a friend of the old man, but it wouldn't do her any good. Vito was still calling all the shots.

'Ah, my beautiful English Lily,' Giovanni said, pushing himself up against the ornate carved headboard.

'I hope you haven't been waiting,' Lily said, hurrying across the room to help him with his pillows.

'I always wait for you.' Giovanni smiled, and Lily knew it wasn't a reprimand. Over the last few weeks, her visits to *Ca' Salvatore* had become a daily event that they both enjoyed.

However, during her mother's stay she'd only popped in once, briefly. It had been clear that the instant rapport she'd shared with Giovanni was not present between her mother and the old gentleman.

'My mum is flying home today.' Lily glanced at her watch. 'In fact, she's probably on a plane right now.'

'That's good,' Giovanni said. 'Now you can spend more time with your husband.'

Lily blinked and stared at him, momentarily lost for words.

'I'm old,' Giovanni said. 'I don't have the time to pussyfoot around, watching what I say.'

'Did you ever, even when you were young?' Lily laughed, despite the fact his instruction to spend more time with Vito had unsettled her. She liked Giovanni, and couldn't ever imagine being offended by him, no matter how directly he spoke. But of course he didn't know—he could *never* know—the truth behind her marriage to Vito.

'Hmm.' He pretended to pause and think. 'Not so much.' He flashed a winning smile at her, momentarily taking years off his age. 'But I'm serious.'

'Vito's been very busy,' Lily prevaricated, letting her gaze drift across the fabulous fresco that decorated the wall. 'Work…'

'I can see you love him, and that he loves you.' Giovanni spoke with assurance. 'But there is tension between you.'

'Well…' Lily's words dried up because she had no idea how to respond. Giovanni had seen love where there simply wasn't any. Vito's feelings for her were obviously the complete opposite of love—he'd made that plain enough. And, although she had once foolishly believed she was falling in love with him, now, after the awful things he'd said and the dreadful way he'd treated her, she'd be crazy to open her heart to him again.

'*You* must fix it now,' Giovanni said. 'My grandson is a good man. But he is proud. He won't make the first move.'

'I'll talk to him,' Lily promised, because there was nothing else she could say.

Lily walked through the twisting maze of alleys, past the fabulous jewellery shops and Venetian trinket-stores, deep in thought.

Even her favourite *gelateria*, which she often stopped at on her way home, did not catch her attention. Even though she was hungry, and ice cream was one of her favourite foods, she didn't feel like eating. She was thinking about the promise she'd made to Giovanni.

She was also thinking about her mother.

Living her life according to Reggie Morton's rules had taken a terrible toll on Ellen. She'd lost her confidence and her independence. Finally she'd become so scared of life that she'd buried herself in project after project, which in turn had left her preoccupied and unable to have a proper relationship with her daughter.

That was what scared Lily the most. She loved her mother, and knew that she was loved in return, but Ellen hadn't even realised that Lily was facing the biggest crisis of her life. There was no way that she was going to let her child grow up like she had—with no father, and with a mother who'd had her spirit eroded away to the point where she couldn't communicate meaningfully with her daughter.

Lily had married Vito for the sake of her baby. Nothing had changed about that. But Vito still refused to acknowledge the baby and, if she didn't do something to make him see the truth soon, before she knew it she'd be out on her own again with no further chance to talk to him.

She took a deep breath and steeled herself to have a proper conversation with Vito—whether he wanted to or not.

Vito was late home from the office that night. He opened the door of the bedroom quietly, expecting to see Lily lying still as a mouse in bed and pretending to be asleep. Instead he was surprised to see her sitting in a comfortable chair, reading one of her paperback books. She put the book aside and stood up immediately, automatically smoothing her hands down the lightweight fabric of her cappuccino-coloured dress.

'We need to talk,' she said, pushing her sleek blonde hair behind her and straightening her shoulders.

'What about?' Vito crossed the room without breaking his stride and tossed his jacket onto a chair.

'About us,' Lily said. 'About our marriage.'

'There's *no* "us",' he said curtly.

'But there is *our* baby,' Lily said.

'I thought you understood never to make that claim again.' Vito reached up and tugged his silk tie off jerkily. He could feel his anger at her betrayal rising once more. 'I won't tell you again.'

'Why won't you give me a chance?' She sounded calm, but Vito could see the colour warming her cheeks.

'Because you betrayed me.'

'When you proposed you said it was for the baby's sake,' she appealed to him. 'But that was a lie. You know how horrible it was for me, always knowing my father didn't want me. How can you do that to your own baby? It's unforgivable.'

'It's *not* my baby,' Vito grated.

The heartfelt emotion in her voice scratched down his nerves like nails on a chalkboard. *She* was the one who had done the unforgivable. Everything he had done was for his family—for his grandfather's sake.

'I don't know what else to say to convince you.' Lily stared at him, a feeling of helplessness suddenly looming up through her misery.

If she could never prove her innocence to him, what was the point of her staying in Venice? Had she made a mistake staying so long?

Should she give up the fight to make Vito realize he *was* the father of her baby, go back to London, and see if her old boss, Mike, would let her try out for that job? If only she hadn't given up the opportunity when it had been available to her.

'Don't say anything,' Vito said. He was studying her

in return, and she could see the tension evident in every plane of his face. 'I keep telling you that.'

'I just wish there was something I could do to make you believe that I wasn't unfaithful,' she said. 'If only I knew *why* you think you're not the father…'

His blue eyes were cast into shadow by brows that were drawn low, but she saw a flash of emotion suddenly flare within them. Emotion so raw it was as painful to witness as it must have been to feel. Then, as she stared up at him, a muscle started pulsing stubbornly beneath the dark stubble on his jawbone.

Without thinking she lifted her hand to touch his face.

A shock wave of sexual awareness surged through her, and she snatched her hand back. But not before she'd seen an answering glint in Vito's eyes.

'Can't we move past this anger and mistrust?' she asked, trying to speak calmly, despite the way her heart was beating out a furious tattoo in response to the sizzling energy that was suddenly flowing between them. 'We can't go back in time and alter what's already happened between us—but we could try to get along. Maybe then you'll be able to trust me again.'

Perhaps she was being too honest, too open about her desire to see Vito acknowledge his child. But it was dishonesty and lies that had led them to this impasse, where it seemed impossible to get through to him, and pointless for her to stay with him.

'What are you doing now?' Vito asked, his sensual lips spreading into a predatorial smile. 'You failed to convince me with your emotional appeal, so now you're trying to tempt me with another more basic form of persuasion?'

'No, I'd never do that!' Lily gasped, feeling her cheeks flame as she realised what Vito was implying.

'You're not offering sex as a way to manipulate me?' He stepped closer and lifted his hand to mimic Lily's earlier action. Except when a frisson leapt between them he didn't withdraw his hand—he pushed it further, slipping his fingers deep into her silky hair.

A shiver skittered through Lily as her body responded instantly to Vito's touch. But she couldn't let him continue to think the worst about her in every way.

'All I meant was maybe we could try to patch things up between us, find a way to build bridges. End the hostility between us.'

'I'd like to build bridges,' Vito said, sliding his free hand around her waist, and pulling her hard up against him so that she could feel his erection pushing against her. She knew what kind of bridge between them he wanted to build—and she wanted it too.

'No, that's not what this is about,' Lily said, despite the way her body was trembling with sudden, urgent desire for Vito. 'I'm just trying to find a way we can reach a truce—find a way to communicate.'

'You're right—we always communicated best through sex,' Vito murmured, leaning close so that his words tickled her ear. He paused to push her blonde hair aside and pressed his lips against the sensitive skin of her neck.

'That's not what I meant.' She drew in a shuddering breath and tried to keep her voice steady as she spoke, but it was difficult with Vito's tongue flicking a delicious trail down towards her collarbone.

'It doesn't matter what you meant,' Vito said, putting both arms around her. 'It's what you want. What we both want.'

'Yes.' Lily couldn't fight the tide of rising passion any longer. She didn't want to fight any more. She closed her eyes and leant into his embrace.

Anticipation coiled deep within her and, almost without conscious thought, she lifted her arms to loop them about his neck and tilted her face towards him. He responded in a heartbeat, bringing his mouth down over hers.

His tongue swept past her open lips and she felt herself start to melt in his arms. She kissed him back, revelling in the sinuous feel of his tongue against hers, marvelling in the glorious flood of sensations that washed through her body.

She lifted her hands to cup his face, and gently caressed his stubbled jawline with her fingertips. The feel of his masculine features beneath her fingers was intoxicating. She wanted to touch him all over, run her hands over his body in a way that she knew would drive him mad with desire—but not before she had driven herself wild with growing need.

She pulled back from his kiss breathlessly, and gazed up into his gorgeous face through a haze of longing. He was still holding her close, his hands buried deep in her long, loose hair, and for a moment she was lost in the darkening depths of his blue eyes. Then in one smooth movement he took hold of her zip and pulled it all the way down her sensitive spine.

She shivered in response, waiting to feel his hands slip inside her dress and caress her back, but instead he brought his hands up to ease the dress off her shoulders and pull the front down so that her lacy bra was revealed.

'Your breasts are even fuller,' Vito murmured, tracing their shape through the lace then reaching behind her to undo the fastening.

'A little, I think,' Lily agreed, hearing the breath catch in her throat as Vito cast the flimsy undergarment away. He guided her backwards and pushed her down so that she

was sitting on the edge of the bed. Then he knelt between her knees and took one tingling nipple into his hot mouth.

'Oh!' Lily cried out. Either pregnancy had made her breasts even more sensitive than usual, or her body had gone too long without Vito's exquisite attention. But, whatever the case, wonderful sensations swirled out from her breasts, filling her body with a mounting, shuddering need for more.

As if he sensed her need—which of course he did, Vito always seemed to know exactly what her body craved—he pressed in further between her legs, and lifted the skirt of her dress up over her hips.

His tongue was still moving deliciously against one hard nipple, filling her with wonder at the incredible feelings he was creating. She hardly noticed when, without breaking away, he tugged her briefs down and tossed them to one side.

A second later he released her nipple and dropped down between her legs.

'Vito!' Lily gasped as she realised what he was doing, but at that moment his mouth came into contact with her most intimate feminine flesh.

It wasn't the first time he had kissed her there, had worked his tongue so expertly against the tingling epicentre of her desire. But her body had never responded with such an instant maelstrom of overwhelming sensation.

Her breath was suddenly coming in short, panting gasps and every conscious thought was driven from her mind. All she was aware of was a building crescendo of hot, demanding passion. It was almost too much to bear—but at the same time she couldn't get enough of it.

She writhed beneath his mouth, trying to lift her hands to hold onto his head, but her arms were caught up in a tangle of fabric, still trapped in the sleeves of her dress. There was nothing she could do but lose herself on the spiralling rush of sensation that was surging through her.

Vito lifted his hands to cup her breasts and she cried out again, letting herself fall backwards onto the bed, as wave after wave of pure bliss crashed over her and through her, carrying her on and on in an orgasm that was more powerful than any she had experienced before.

But it wasn't over yet. She had barely floated down from the pinnacle when Vito was moving over her. Somehow he had divested himself of his clothes and he lifted her further up the bed, freeing her arms in the process.

He positioned himself above her, then without hesitation he plunged deep into her already quivering body.

A sound she didn't recognise moaned from her lips, and she gave herself over once again to a miracle of extraordinary pleasure. She lifted her knees and tilted her hips, desperate to feel his hard flesh filling her to capacity. She clung onto him, his muscled shoulders bunching beneath her fingers as he rocked backwards and forwards.

Vito's head dipped against her neck, and she could feel his breath coming in hot, harsh bursts in time with every powerful thrust. Her own breathing was also keeping time with his strong rhythm—high, panting moans that revealed just how lost she was on the rush of uninhibited passion that was storming her body.

Her inner muscles were clenching hard around him, sensation was bursting through her, and once again she felt herself tipping over the edge of utter, all-consuming pleasure.

'Vito!' She cried out his name, then she felt her breath catch in her throat and she was sobbing, saying his name over and over again.

Her head was thrown back against the pillow and her eyes were squeezed shut, but tears were flowing freely down her face as her body trembled in the throes of another orgasm that seemed to go on for ever.

Then suddenly she heard a shout as Vito came to his climax. He reared up above her, his body stopping still for a long moment. Then he shuddered mightily as he reached his own release.

It took a long time for Lily to come back down to earth. She had never experienced anything so intense before, or responded so quickly and wildly to Vito's love-making.

There'd been hardly any foreplay. She hadn't needed it—or even wanted it. With just one touch she had been ready for him, bursting with desire, desperate for him to make her his again.

He was lying next to her quietly, and as she turned her head she saw he was looking at her. His blue eyes caught hers, and an instant shiver ran through her.

'Was that too rough?' he asked, rolling onto his side and placing his hand gently on her stomach.

Lily frowned, startled when she realised what he meant, and instinctively lifted herself up onto her elbows to look down at her own body. It was a surprise to see the ruin of her dress bunched up and crushed around her waist. It wasn't doing anything to cover her and, in a strange sort of way, it made her naked breasts and the exposed apex at the top of her legs appear even more wanton.

'No, I don't think so,' Lily said. Her eyes were fixed on his large bronzed hand resting lightly on her small, neat bump. She couldn't see his fingers properly as the crumpled dress was obscuring them, but she could feel the heat of his palm against her skin, and it was reawakening her sensual response to him.

'Are *you* all right?' Vito brought his gaze back up to her face, and he lifted his hand to brush her tear-stained cheek.

'Yes,' Lily said stiffly. She suddenly felt exposed and vulnerable in front of Vito. Of course he knew how powerfully she had responded to his love-making, and she was all too aware of how her body was already starting to sing again with renewed desire for him.

'You never cried before,' he said, smoothing her hair back from her damp face.

She stared at him with wide eyes, suddenly realising a momentous truth. She had tried to shut her heart to him— but her body had always remained true to her deeper feelings. It had opened to him, yearned to be one with him.

Because she loved him.

Despite everything, she had never stopped loving him. And if she didn't do something to hide it from him Vito would soon realise the humiliating truth as well.

'Maybe I missed sex,' she quipped, trying to keep her voice as light as her words. 'Or maybe it's pregnancy. They say pregnancy makes you hot.'

Her flippant response was out of character, and she tensed up inside, waiting to see if Vito would challenge her. But how well could he really know her, if he still believed she had been unfaithful to him?

'You were always hot.' In a flash he was kneeling over her, taking hold of her crushed dress and pulling it down over her hips. 'That's better—this is how I like you best. Totally naked, apart from your glorious curly hair.'

'I thought you liked it straightened.' Lily forced herself to reply even though she was crying inside. All he saw was a naked woman to share his bed. All she saw

was the man who would never return her love. 'I always straightened it for you.'

'Why?' Vito asked. He rolled onto his back and lifted her astride him so that her long, loose hair tumbled down over her shoulders and pooled on his broad chest. 'What made you think that?'

'Something you said—a compliment you paid me,' Lily replied, remembering one of their early dates when, despite his reluctance to behave like a tourist in his own city, he had taken her on a gondola. He had pulled her into his arms and run his hands through her hair, saying it was as smooth as spun gold and looked like a liquid sunrise reflected in the lagoon on a glorious winter dawn.

'I don't remember.' Vito's dismissive words cut into her like a knife. She had made a habit of straightening her hair based on cherished words of flattery he had spoken to her. But it had all been meaningless to him. 'This is how I like it now,' he continued. 'Wild and wanton, like you.'

Lily looked down, letting her hair fall forward to shield her expression.

She'd just realised the most monumental fact—she loved Vito. And yet at every turn she saw again and again just how little she meant to him.

'We have a lot of time to make up for.' The words caught in Lily's throat, but she hoped he'd mistake her shaky tone for rising passion. If she was going to survive in this marriage she had to find a way to shield her heart and her true feelings from him.

'What do you want to do now?' Vito asked, running his hands over the curve of her hips and snuggling her closer to his erection.

'No more talking,' Lily said, dipping her body forward to run her tongue over the sensitive skin of his throat. Her nipples tightened as they brushed against his chest, and desire was already building within her, mercifully blotting out the pain in her heart.

She couldn't bear to hear any more words that made her realise how little she'd meant to him, even back when she'd thought they were happy. Before he believed she'd betrayed him.

He had been everything to her. He still was.

CHAPTER NINE

LILY was still asleep the following morning as Vito dressed for work. He moved quietly around the room so that he didn't disturb her. It was the first time since he'd brought her back to Venice that he'd seen her in a really deep sleep. Most mornings when he'd got ready for work she'd already been up. And most evenings, even if she'd been in bed pretending to be asleep, she'd been restless.

She made a small sound and rolled over, reaching above her head to flip the pillow over, then snuggled back down, surrounded by a wild mass of long blonde curls.

Vito smiled, recognising the action. Even in her sleep she liked the cold side of the pillow. She was such a warm-blooded creature that she always liked cool things. Iced water, ice cream. And now that she was pregnant it was like a tiny furnace was glowing inside her. He wondered how she would cope as the summer heated up. He'd take her away to his estate on the Veneto plain. Or even up to his retreat in the Dolomite mountains. But he'd need to keep her medical care in mind—he couldn't allow anything to happen to her or the baby.

He gazed down at her. Possibly for the first time in months he really let himself look, safe in the knowledge that she was oblivious to his attention. She was lying on her side with one knee drawn up and the other leg stretched out. She looked like a graceful gazelle, frozen at the height of an elegant leap.

An unexpected feeling prickled through him, and he acknowledged it for what it was: he'd missed Lily, missed what he thought they'd had together before he'd discovered her betrayal.

This marriage was all about doing what was right for his grandfather—Giovanni deserved to reach the end of his life knowing that his legacy would go on.

But if things continued like last night—their love-making had been nothing short of incendiary—it was going to be much more pleasant than he'd thought when they were still at daggers drawn.

Lily slept late that morning, and when she awoke her body was filled with the languid glow of complete sensual satisfaction. She rolled over and stretched, noticing the time with surprise. But, after the utter lack of inhibition she'd shown with Vito the night before, she was pleased he'd already left for work. She wasn't entirely sure that she was ready to face him yet.

She made her way to the *en suite* and ran herself a deep, luxurious bath. With her hair piled haphazardly on top of her head, she lay back in the soft bubbles and thought about what had happened with Vito. She could feel a blush rising to her cheeks as she remembered how wildly she'd behaved with him. His touch had sent her up in flames. They'd made love before—many, many times. But it had never been so intense.

Maybe that had been her body's way of letting her know that she loved him.

Up until last night her mind had certainly rejected that possibility, after the way he had treated her. But perhaps it was impossible to change the reality of her deeper feelings simply by telling herself what she ought to believe. Her heart still knew the truth.

However, she knew that loving him made her vulnerable. A small sigh escaped her as she stepped out of the bath onto the marble mosaic floor. She must *never* let him guess the depth of her feelings.

She dried herself briskly and set about getting dressed for her visit to Giovanni. She liked to wear something nice for him. He didn't see many people, and he often complimented her on her appearance.

Suddenly she caught sight of herself in the mirror, and stopped and stared. Her eyes were shining brightly, her cheeks were flushed, and her hair was bouncing wildly about her shoulders in a riot of curls.

She couldn't visit Giovanni looking that that! The sharp-witted old man would guess immediately what had caused such a change in the way she looked. She'd simply feel too self-conscious—like a deflowered virgin the morning after her wedding night, wondering if everyone knew what she had just experienced for the first time.

She sat down at the dressing table and pulled her ceramic straighteners from the drawer. Then she hesitated. Vito had said he liked her hair curly. If she straightened it again, it would seem like she was making the point that she didn't care about his opinion. But, on the other hand, she definitely didn't want to make it appear that she would do anything to please him—she'd already been down that route when she'd started straightening her hair because of an apparently meaningless comment he didn't even remember making.

In the end she did her hair in the same smooth style she'd worn since returning to Venice. She was already late for Giovanni, and she couldn't let herself waste time worrying about silly details. She had more important things to concern her, like whether the old man would ask her straight out if she'd managed to ease the tension that he had detected between her and Vito.

As it turned out she need not have worried. Giovanni was tired that day and spent most of her visit dozing. When he was awake he told her about the great flood of 1966. It had been more than forty years ago, but his memories were sharp and his descriptions vivid as he told her how the sea level had risen by two metres, washing right through the ground floor of *Ca' Salvatore*, and causing untold damage to the city.

Walking back home to the *palazzo*, Lily reflected on her new friendship with Giovanni. He was old, and according to his doctors did not have long to live, but Lily was so grateful for the time she was able to spend with him. He had accepted her so warmly into his family, and his personal stories about his life and the city that had always been his home meant a lot to her.

Whatever happened with Vito, in years to come she would tell her child how happy Giovanni had been, knowing his grandchild was on the way. She would remember the stories he had told her, so that her child would know about his or her Italian family—even if Vito still refused to acknowledge them.

Vito paced back and forth across his study impatiently. He'd come home to see Lily, but she hadn't returned from her daily visit to his grandfather.

She was late. And he wanted to see her now.

He'd spent the morning totally distracted, until finally he'd given into his desire to come home and ravish her.

Sex with Lily had always been good, but last night they had taken it to a new level. It had been utterly mind-blowing, and he hadn't been able to stop thinking about it all morning. Thinking about doing it again and again.

He strode over to the window, cursing himself for his lack of control.

Why was he letting Lily get to him so badly? Was it simply that he'd been too long without a woman, and now last night had reminded his body what it had been missing?

He looked at his watch, wondering again what time she would return. Perhaps he should go out in search of her, but although *Ca' Salvatore* wasn't far away there were several routes she could take home.

Suddenly he found himself questioning why she kept visiting Giovanni even though she knew there was no future in it. What did she hope to gain, either for herself or for her child?

He hadn't stopped her visits because his grandfather seemed to really enjoy them. But it puzzled him that Lily genuinely seemed to enjoy them too.

She wasn't like the other women he'd known. That was part of what had attracted him to her in the first place.

She really didn't seem interested in his wealth and status. Spending time together was all she'd ever really wanted from him.

The thought troubled him, but he pushed it to the back of his mind. He sat down at his desk and opened his laptop, determined to get himself back under control.

It was later than usual when Lily got home. As she climbed the stairs to the first floor of the *palazzo*, a strange feeling prickled down her spine, as if she was being watched.

'I've been waiting for you.'

Startled, despite the fact her senses had warned her Vito was close, she stopped mid-step and looked up to see him standing outside his study.

The sight of him lounging nonchalantly against the door-jamb, oozing self-assurance and sex appeal from every inch of his incredible body, sent her pulse racing. Her breath caught in her throat and she felt butterflies start to flutter wildly in her stomach.

'I've been to see your grandfather.' The words sounded husky and she swallowed, determined to keep her cool, even though her body and mind were suddenly beset by vivid memories of their wild love-making the night before.

'How was he?' His silky Italian accent shimmied straight through her defences, and her composure started to dissolve immediately.

'Fine, but very tired. He told me all about the flood.' She started walking up the stairs towards him, and although she tried she simply couldn't drag her eyes away from him standing in the doorway.

She watched him remove the jacket of his dark suit and loosen his tie. The effect was alarmingly dynamic— as if he didn't intend to keep his immaculate appearance for long. As if he meant business—a different kind of business from usual.

He combed his fingers through his black hair, sweeping it back from his perfectly proportioned face. His skin was lightly bronzed, and he looked the embodiment of health and vigour.

His blue eyes were intense, locked in his unbroken appraisal of her. She felt her skin warming in response to his gaze, yet despite that warmth a shiver began at the nape of her neck and tingled all the way down her backbone.

She reached the top step and still he towered over her,

shamelessly occupying her personal space. In a moment of nervousness she thought she should carry on walking, move past him, but it was strangely difficult to move— or be aware of anything other than Vito. The heat of his body burned through her dress, the sound of his breathing caressed her ears.

Maybe this was *his* personal space, she pondered vaguely. It was his scent that enclosed her, his scent that she pulled deep inside her with every breath she drew.

The potent mix of raw masculinity laced with his exotic cologne, the very essence of the man himself, was making her feel dizzy. She found herself swaying.

His hands closed on her waist. The impact was instant. His sharp intake of breath told her he felt it too—like a surge of electricity zinging between them. He lifted her up the final step and stood her directly before him.

Her head fell back and her eyes widened as she looked up at his face, only inches from her own. His eyes narrowed as his gaze swept over her, settling possessively on her mouth, conveying his thoughts with devastating certainty.

She was breathing quickly in small, shaky bursts through slightly parted lips. Her tongue peeked out treacherously, moistening lips that were already red, and tingling in willful anticipation of his kiss, betraying her needs to him.

'I came home to make love to you.'

His words seared through her like a liquid fire, melting the last of her defences, whipping up the flames of her desire. She stared up at him with wide eyes, knowing that just how much she wanted him must be written all over her face.

Suddenly he stepped backwards, pulling her into his

study with him. The door banged shut and he turned the key. Then he brought all his attention back to her.

'I couldn't get last night out of my mind,' he said, tugging her close to him.

'I thought about it too.' Lily's voice wavered. His hands had already found the tiny pearl buttons that fastened the front of her dress and he was making quick work of them.

'It was incredible,' Vito said, gripping the hem of her dress and pulling it straight over the top of her head. He tossed the garment aside, then his hands were on her naked skin, sweeping across her body in a way that set her trembling deep inside.

Lily gazed at him through a growing haze of sexual excitement. He was utterly gorgeous and he was going to make love to her. Her heart was racing and her legs felt weak. Just like last night, all it had taken was the merest touch and her body was on fire for him again.

She lifted her hands, tugging distractedly at his clothing. He knew what she wanted, and within moments he was standing naked before her.

Her eyes roamed greedily over his magnificent body, revelling in his pure masculine perfection, before being drawn inexorably to the proud thrust of his erection.

She wanted to touch. Needed to touch. Without a conscious decision she reached for him and her fingers coiled around his hard, jutting flesh.

'Lily!' He closed his eyes and a deep, feral sound rumbled from within his chest. Then, never taking her eyes off his face, she began to move her hand in the way she knew he liked.

His breathing changed immediately, and he dragged air into his lungs in an uneven rhythm through parted lips. His head had dipped to one side, letting his fringe fall forward, and she saw his tongue flick against his teeth.

Suddenly she ached to kiss him. Without letting go of him, she stepped closer. Then, standing on tiptoes, she pulled his head down to hers.

He kissed her hungrily, his tongue plunging into her mouth with an erotic intimacy, and all the while she was aware of her hand caressing him, felt his reaction to the movement of her fingers through his kiss.

Suddenly he pulled away, gasping for breath, and gripped her wrist to still her hand.

'No more. Not now.' His voice was as laboured as his breathing, and she knew what he meant. He wanted this to last for both of them.

Almost reluctantly she uncoiled her fingers, but then he pulled her close and spun her round in front of him, so that he could lift her hair out of the way and kiss the back of her neck.

'You are so beautiful,' he murmured, before tracing the edge of her ear with his tongue.

She trembled and leant back against him, the skin of her back pressed against the skin of his chest. And the whole time she was acutely conscious of the length of his erection behind her.

'Look in the mirror,' he murmured. 'See what I see.'

She lifted her eyes and stared at their reflection in his large mirror. He was behind her, curled over her possessively, and she was standing in her lacy bra and briefs surrounded by a shimmering curtain of blonde hair.

Suddenly his hands began to slide around to the front of her body.

It was a strange sensation to feel and watch at the same time as his large bronzed hand slipped beneath the lace of her bra. Her nipple tightened to a hard point against his palm, then suddenly he eased the stretch-lace down so that her breast came free of the bra cup.

She gasped as erotic feelings flooded through her. Supported and lifted underneath, her breast thrust proudly towards the mirror, the nipple a pert, rosy bud that drew the eye.

'Is that uncomfortable?' he asked, his breath tickling her ear so that she shivered and tilted her head towards him.

'No.' She shook her head, aware of her breast, of the way her nipple felt supercharged with the aching need to be touched.

His hand slipped beneath her other breast, lifting it out of the bra cup as well. Now both breasts were pointing shamelessly towards the mirror, tight and tingling with the need to feel Vito's hands on them.

She didn't have to wait any longer. Vito brought his palms up to knead them both gently in a way that made her moan and arch back in encouragement. When his fingers teased her nipples she gasped and closed her eyes, pressing her head back against his shoulders.

'Look in the mirror,' he whispered huskily. 'You are so beautiful.'

She opened her eyes in time to see his right hand release her breast and slide downwards, across her stomach, then lower still.

She held her breath, pure sexual excitement coursing through her as she anticipated his masterful touch. Her skin was flushed, and she could see a wild light in her eyes. Then his fingers slipped beneath the lace of her briefs, quickly locating the centre of her desire, and she was lost on a sudden rush of sensation.

It an instant her body was engulfed by marvellous feelings that pulsed right through her. She moaned, leaning back against his strong chest, and he continued to caress her, sending her higher and higher.

She rocked her hips, moving jerkily against his hand

as the feelings became increasingly intense. She twisted in his arms, almost as if she wanted to get away. But that was the last thing she wanted. He'd carried her up to the brink. And now she needed the ultimate release from the pressure building within her.

As if to prove how perfectly in tune their bodies were, he let her go for a moment to pull her briefs down. Then he bent her over his huge leather topped desk.

She barely had time to register his intention when she felt him pressing close behind her. Her legs were slightly apart, and she let herself flop forward so that her forearms were resting on the desk. He took hold of her hips to steady her, and with one expert thrust was inside her.

Her breath whooshed out of her as a sudden rush of pleasure washed through her. She felt alive and tingling in every part of her body. But as he started to move, pulling out and stroking back in, she was soon lost on a rising tide of overwhelming sensation.

Her heart was racing beneath her breast and her blood was singing in her ears. There was no room for conscious thought as her body was overtaken by the incredible experience of feeling Vito moving inside her.

She leant on the desk, resting her head on her arms, buried in a cascade of blonde hair. Vito was holding her from behind, tugging her close so they were joined as tightly as possible on each thrust. Her legs were as weak as water, but she didn't realise that Vito was holding her up.

She was only aware of the marvellous upward spiral of growing ecstasy within her, until suddenly she reached the pinnacle and her world exploded in a beautiful, climatic release.

With a perfect mastery of timing, Vito followed

straight after her, crying her name, and dragged her tighter still. Then his body shuddered and convulsed with his own powerful orgasm.

Lily lay against his chest on the leather sofa in his study, wrapped in a gorgeous warm glow of sexual satisfaction. She had never expected to come home to such an incredible experience—but she certainly wasn't complaining.

Vito was still naked—as was she, apart from her lacy bra. In a moment of self-consciousness, she had slipped her breasts back inside the cups. But, considering the fact she hadn't replaced her briefs or done anything else to cover her nakedness, she was still feeling amazingly relaxed.

'We've wasted too much time,' Vito said, running his fingertips idly up her long, creamy thigh.

'We can make up for it.' Lily smiled at him shyly. 'Especially if you come home for lunch every day.'

'This isn't my lunch break,' Vito said, letting his gaze slide over her body in a way that made her heart skip a beat. He slipped his hand under her thigh and lifted her leg over his lap, so that once again she was open for his touch. 'I'm not going back to the office today. I've taken the afternoon off.'

Lily looked up at him, amazingly feeling the heat of longing wash through her once more despite the fact that she'd felt totally satisfied a moment ago.

'How can you do that to me, with just a look?' she whispered, aware that a rosy flush of excitement was spreading over her skin again.

'Do what?' he teased, raising one hand to lift a swathe of her long blonde hair back over her shoulder so that her bra was showing. Her nipples jutted jauntily beneath the transparent stretch-lace, as if they were seeking his attention.

'Set me on fire,' she said shakily. 'Make me ache for you with every fibre of my being.'

'Maybe because that's how looking at you affects me too.' He lifted his hands to hold her face tenderly and she looked deep into his blue eyes, knowing that what he said was true.

Right at that second, Lily knew that they had just shared a powerful moment. It felt like the first time they had been totally honest with each other.

She knew it was only about one aspect of their relationship—the physical side. But that was important. She felt so much closer to Vito than she'd felt yesterday. And maybe now they would continue to grow closer still, each time they made love.

'I don't even need to look at you to want you,' Vito said, trailing his fingers deliciously down her collarbone. 'Just thinking about you makes me hard. This morning in the office I couldn't do a stroke of work.'

'Really?' Lily asked shyly. She'd always thought of Vito as totally in control, whatever situation he was in.

'Enough conversation.' Vito's voice was deep and gravelly as he suddenly pulled her round so she was sitting astride him. 'This time I'm going to take it slowly.'

CHAPTER TEN

'THANK you for coming with me,' Lily said. She blinked in the bright light as they left the hospital after her mid-pregnancy scan.

'You don't need to thank me.' Vito held her hand as she stepped down into the boat. 'It was my duty to be there.'

Lily squinted up at him, but she couldn't read his expression through the glare reflected off the water. During the scan he had seemed cold and distant, which was not how he'd been with her generally over the last couple of weeks. Since the night they'd made love things had been so different—much warmer, with almost no tension between them at all.

But that was probably because all they did together was make love, she thought with a hint of sadness. At first she'd been overwhelmed by their new-found intimacy and enjoyment of each other. He was the most amazing, generous lover, and he treated her like a princess.

Just looking at him made her heart skip a beat, and the love that she'd finally admitted she felt for him had continued to grow, like a precious secret in her heart. But as time went by she needed more. She wanted to be able to do more together than have sex.

Of course that was wonderful—but it would also be

wonderful to be able to talk to him, have a proper conversation. She was aware that whenever her comments became more than just pillow talk he found a way to silence her. Perhaps with a kiss, or a caress, or with a suggestion of something exquisite he'd like to do with her willing body.

'Did you mind it when I asked the radiographer the sex of the baby?' She delved in her handbag for her sunglasses. She wanted to be able to look at him properly, to see if she could detect any clue as to how he was feeling after the scan.

'My grandfather will be pleased that you are carrying a boy.' His tone was bland and did not reveal anything about his mood.

She found her sunglasses and put them on, then her eyes came to rest on the scan photos she had tucked carefully into her bag.

'Do you want one of these?' she asked, holding the flimsy pictures tightly, as the boat was moving and a stiff breeze was blowing.

'I'm sure my grandfather would like to see them *all*.' He pulled his mobile phone out of his pocket and switched it on to check if he'd missed any calls or emails while they'd been inside the hospital. 'Put them away to keep them safe.'

Lily gazed at him quietly. His black hair was whipping about and the jacket of his suit was billowing slightly in the wind—but his face was set in stone. He didn't look angry. In fact he looked completely devoid of emotion.

It must be hard for him, she knew, believing the child inside her was not his. She still didn't know why he thought that, but after the wonderful accord they seemed to have reached lately, at least in the bedroom, it seemed *so* wrong that he still believed something that simply wasn't true.

A few minutes later they were travelling along the Grand Canal. Even though she had been there many times before, Lily couldn't help being impressed by the magnificent array of buildings that edged the water. Recently Giovanni had started to tell her some of the history surrounding many of the important families that had owned the *palazzi* that could be seen from his bedroom window. She'd found it absolutely fascinating.

'It's already late morning, so I thought you might like to stop at *Ca' Salvatore*,' Vito said. 'Unless you're tired and you'd like me to take you home before I go to the office?'

'No, I'd like to visit Giovanni,' Lily said. 'I want to see his face when he learns he is to have a great-grandson.' She glanced at Vito, suddenly feeling slightly awkward. The comparison between his grandfather's pleasure and Vito's utter lack of interest was uncomfortably obvious.

'He'll probably start choosing names. Traditional family names, suitable for the newest Salvatore,' Vito said. 'But don't be concerned. We won't name the child anything you are not happy with.'

Lily pushed her hair back off her face and looked at him with interest. Just when she thought he was showing as much emotion and understanding as one of the marble statues at *Ca' Salvatore*, he took her by surprise. It was the first time he'd said anything that showed he took her feelings into account.

'I'd like to choose a name that makes Giovanni happy,' she said. She wasn't worried about Giovanni's choice of names for her son. To tell the truth, it touched her deeply to know that her son was truly wanted by his great-grandfather, and was important enough to be included in the family tradition of names. But in the circumstances it was a bittersweet thought. If only Vito felt the same way as his grandfather.

'I'll be late tonight,' Vito said, jumping out of the boat to offer Lily a steadying hand as she disembarked at the water entrance of *Ca' Salvatore*. 'I have a lot to catch up on.'

Lily watched as the boat eased back out into the traffic on the Grand Canal. She'd felt so happy during the scan, seeing images of her baby. But now a heavy weight of sadness was descending on her.

The past couple of weeks had been wonderful, spending time with Vito again. She had pushed her concerns about the future to the back of her mind, telling herself that the intimacy she had rediscovered with him would help rebuild the trust between them.

But this morning his reaction to the scan had told her nothing had changed. Even the awe-inspiring sight of a tiny baby growing inside her hadn't softened him. By his actions he'd made it very clear that he was just as hard-hearted towards her as ever.

The next few weeks continued in the same way. It seemed impossible for Lily to spend any time with Vito without ending up in his arms.

But she was falling ever more deeply in love with him, and a tiny seed of hope was steadily growing within her heart. If only she could convince him of her innocence maybe things could be genuinely good between them—both in and out of the bedroom.

At last, as her pregnancy advanced, life gradually began to settle into a routine similar to when Lily had first come to Venice to live with Vito. He started taking her out around the city and eating with her in restaurants again, finally giving her the opportunity to talk to him.

But, although it was what she had been hoping so for weeks, she knew she had to be careful to take things slowly, to keep their conversations on neutral ground. She was trying to build the foundations of her unborn baby's life while she had the chance. She couldn't risk ruining everything she was working towards with a rash comment.

Then one evening she was surprised to find herself being guided into Luigi's. It was the first time they had visited the restaurant since their terrible argument when Vito had been horribly suspicious of the kindly restaurateur.

She stiffened unconsciously as they crossed the threshold. It was unbearable that he had brought her here, especially after they had been getting on so well. Luigi was bound to say something, and she didn't know how Vito would react.

'Lily, Vito!' Luigi bundled over to them with an extravagant flourish. 'It is wonderful to see you again after so long.'

'Luigi.' Vito greeted the proprietor of the restaurant with a neutral tone.

'*Mamma mia!* I see congratulations are in order!' he exclaimed as his gaze settled on Lily's very obvious bump.

'Thank you.' Vito guided Lily to her chair and held it for her himself.

'And I am so glad to see you back in Venice after the last time we met,' Luigi said, addressing his first words to Lily. Then he turned to Vito, a protective glint flashing unexpectedly in his eye. 'You must have been so worried, to think that your love was roaming the streets alone that cold, foggy night.'

It was the comment Lily had been dreading. She couldn't stand it. She'd worked so hard to make things right with Vito—for the sake of her unborn son and also for her own future happiness. Suddenly, at that awful moment, it seemed easier to bear the shame herself rather than have Luigi think the worst of Vito.

'It was a silly misunderstanding,' Lily blurted.

'No, it was my responsibility.' Vito spoke calmly and placed his hand over Lily's, which lay trembling on the white-linen tablecloth. 'And I wish to thank you for taking care of Lily when I was remiss.'

'You must be so pleased to have her back,' Luigi said. He still had an assessing look in his eye, making Lily want to move the conversation on as quickly as possible.

'It's—good to be here.' She stumbled over her reply.

'She's my wife now,' Vito added, his voice deep and intense.

'*Molte congratulazioni!*' Luigi beamed, instantly loosing all of his sternness. He called across to a waiter to bring out a bottle of prosecco.

Lily felt Vito's hand pressing hers, and she lifted her gaze to his face. He looked as drop-dead gorgeous as ever, but she couldn't read his expression. Was he telling her that he believed that she had not been involved with Luigi?

Or was he simply letting her understand that, despite the fact that he believed she had been unfaithful—if not with Luigi, then with some one else—this was all part of the act he was prepared to play to ensure his grandfather's happiness?

But, as glasses of sparkling prosecco were poured, and extravagant Italian toasts to the newlyweds were made, she couldn't dwell on the problem any longer.

* * *

'You look terrible,' Vito said, rushing to help her up the last few stairs and onto the sofa in his study.

'Thanks.' Lily tried to smile, but she really didn't feel very well.

'I'll call the doctor,' Vito said, dropping down onto one knee in front of her to look at her properly.

'There's no need,' Lily said. 'I only went for a check-up two days ago. Everything's fine—it's just I got so hot walking back from *Ca' Salvatore*.'

With a muffled curse Vito shot across the room to the bar area, clunked ice into a tumbler and poured mineral water on top.

'I'm sorry,' he said as he handed the glass to her. 'I should have thought of bringing you something to drink right away.'

'That's all right,' Lily said, touched by his concern. 'The first thing I needed was just to sit down.'

'You shouldn't be walking in this heat,' Vito said. 'You need to rest for a few days. Then, after you are recovered, if you want to visit my grandfather you must go by boat.'

'I don't need a few *days'* rest,' Lily protested. 'I'll be all right by tomorrow. And I need to walk or I won't get any exercise at all, and that can't be good for me.'

'I'm calling the doctor.' From the decisive tone of his voice it was clear that he had already made his mind up. 'I want to know for myself what it is all right for you to do. I won't let you overdo it.'

Lily stared at him in bewildered consternation. At seven months pregnant she could still be working full-time, if she wasn't in the privileged position of being married to a rich man.

'Your ankles are puffy.' Vito knelt down to pull off her

sandals. He sat next to her on the sofa, turned her sideways and lifted her feet up onto his lap. 'Is that normal?'

'I think so,' Lily said as Vito began to stroke gently along her feet, smoothing the slight indentations the straps of her sandals had made, and then massaging up her calves towards her knees. 'Unless it gets too bad. The midwife always checks for it—but I don't know what it means.'

'I'll ask the doctor.'

'Really, I'm fine now,' Lily protested. The glass of water had refreshed her, and she really did feel fine. Better than fine, in fact. The touch of Vito's fingers, which she was certain he meant to be purely comforting, was already doing things to her libido. Her progression well into her third trimester had not done anything to curb her physical desire for Vito. 'But I think I might feel better if I freshen up in the shower.'

Before she realised what he was about, Vito swept her up into his strong arms and, holding her cradled against the broad planes of his chest, carried her upstairs to their bedroom.

He took her through into the *en suite* and set her down on the marble floor. The small mosaic tiles felt deliciously cool under her feet and, as always when she was close to Vito, Lily felt completely aware of her own body. And every inch of her skin or strand of her hair was conscious of Vito—longing to touch or be touched by him.

'Do you need any help?' he asked, and Lily could see from the darkening of his blue eyes that he knew exactly what she needed.

'I'd love some help.' She sucked in a shaky breath as he brushed past her to turn on the shower. Then, bending to take hold of the hem of her loose-fitting summer dress, he pulled it up and straight over her head.

He shed his own clothes quickly, and kicked them out of the door into the bedroom before turning back to her.

'You are so beautiful,' he said, letting his hands caress her seven-month bump as he reached for her lacy underwear.

Lily held onto his powerful shoulders as she stepped out of her briefs. He still showed such adoration of her body, even though her pregnancy was well advanced. And he was very inventive when it came to finding new ways for them to enjoy their love-making despite her changing body. The way he was treating her gave her hope for the future—maybe in time he would come to share her feelings of love.

He reached behind her to unfasten her bra. And then, totally naked, they both stepped into the shower. She sighed as Vito started to smooth exotically scented shower cream over her body. Being with him was incredible.

Later that evening Vito took Lily to his house in the Dolomite mountain-range. As soon as she stepped out of the helicopter she could feel her body relaxing in the cooler atmosphere. Although sometimes it had felt like it, she knew she hadn't really been hot all the time in Venice—the *palazzo* was air-conditioned—but there was something wonderfully refreshing about being in clear mountain air.

'It's incredible,' Lily breathed, gazing at the awe-inspiring view.

'The chalet makes a useful retreat,' Vito agreed. 'And it will be a good place for you to rest.'

'I don't exactly do much in Venice,' Lily protested, turning to look at what she presumed must be Vito's chalet. It didn't look like her idea of a chalet—but then she was thinking of the small, individual holiday-homes she and Ellen had sometimes stayed in while she was growing up. Not an impressive timber building that looked more like an exclusive alpine ski-lodge. 'I'm pregnant—not an invalid.'

'The doctor thought it would be good for you to get out of the city,' Vito said, taking her hand and leading her up the wooden steps to an impressive first-floor balcony that appeared to run right round the building. 'And I agree with him.'

He led her into the first-floor living space, which was laid out to take maximum benefit from the ravishing view that seemed to roll on and on for ever.

'Sit down and rest, while I speak to the housekeeper about dinner.'

Obediently, Lily sunk into a huge comfy armchair. It did feel good to be off her feet, even though she'd only just stepped out of the helicopter. And before that she'd spent most of the afternoon sleeping, until Vito had woken her up to tell her that the doctor had arrived.

He had confirmed that everything was fine, and had said there would be no harm in Lily leaving the city for a while. After he had left, Lily had started to say that there was no need for Vito to disrupt his work routine for her. But then she'd discovered Vito had already packed for her while she'd been asleep.

She knew that once Vito had made up his mind there was no way to change it. And also she was secretly touched that he'd taken the trouble to pack her things himself. Never in her life had anyone packed her suitcase for her. On short breaks away with Ellen, she'd always had to be the responsible one who made sure nothing essential was forgotten.

'I've brought you a drink.' Vito paused in the doorway, holding a glass of iced water in his hand, and watched at her gazing out at the view.

She looked beautiful. There was a gentle glow to her cheeks, and in profile he could see the slightly upturned tip of her delicate nose. Her hair was tied back at the nape of her neck, but long blonde curls had escaped and were coiling prettily around the side of her face.

'Thank you.' She turned to him and smiled, the expression lighting up her already radiant face. Suddenly he was pleased he'd brought her away from the city. He could have her all to himself without any distractions. Soon the child would be born and, although it was the whole point of this marriage, he knew everything would change. Lily would have a new focus in her life, and the pleasant routine they had established would be replaced.

'It seemed a good bet that you'd like a drink—you're always thirsty these days.' He passed her the glass and sat in an armchair, facing her.

'I didn't know about this place,' Lily said, ice-cubes clinking as she took a long drink of water. 'Do you use it often?'

'For skiing in the winter,' Vito said, grimly remembering how he had spent nearly two weeks after Lily had left at Easter hurling himself recklessly down black runs. 'And it makes a quiet place to get away from it all in the summer. It's not too far—even by road—from Venice.'

'You never brought me here,' Lily said. There was a slight crease between her brows as she gazed out at the view.

'It didn't snow until late this year, and then you had

your stomach bug,' Vito said. 'What we *thought* was a stomach bug,' he amended.

'Oh.' Lily put her hand up to smooth her blonde hair. She hesitated self-consciously, as if she'd just realised it was still a riot of curls after their love-making in the shower. He'd left her sleeping in bed, and then there hadn't been time for her to style it in her usual careful way before they'd left the city.

'I do remember saying I liked your hair smooth,' Vito found himself saying. 'It has a beautiful sheen when you straighten it, almost like polished-gold foil embedded in Murano glass.'

Lily was staring at him, her eyes wide with surprise at his confession.

'Then why did you say you didn't like it straightened?' she asked.

'I didn't mean that,' Vito replied, suddenly wishing he hadn't brought the subject up. 'It's just that I prefer it curly.'

'Well, that's good.' Lily put her glass down on the coffee table and stood up to walk across to him. He tilted his head back, looking at her as she perched on the arm of his chair and lifted her hand to run her fingers lightly through his short black hair. 'Because that's how it goes naturally.'

His body responded instantly. It always did. Just looking at her was enough to make him hard with desire. Hell, just *thinking* about her when he was at work was enough. She was gorgeous. Even with her body changing shape, and slowing her down slightly, he still couldn't get enough of her.

'I brought you here to rest.' Looking into her face, he reached up and traced her delicately defined cheekbones with his fingertips. Her eyes glowed with a sultry sexual invitation, and hot desire pulsed through him.

'Then you'd better show me the bedroom,' she said, pulling him to his feet.

Over the next couple of days Lily honestly thought she'd never been so happy in her entire life. She'd made a conscious decision not to let her worries about the future intrude, and she focussed completely on the present, knowing it might be her last opportunity to be truly alone with Vito.

She'd never spent such wonderful, uninterrupted time with him before, and she was revelling in it. As far as she was aware he'd totally ignored his mobile phone and laptop to concentrate entirely on their time together. It was like heaven.

Vito was simply amazing. Attentive to her every need, he looked after her so well, and they visited the most incredible places each day. Then at night he took her in his arms and made wonderful, exquisite love to her.

'You are lucky to have grown up near here.' Lily sighed, rotating on the spot to enjoy the breathtaking panoramic view. Vito had brought her to a beautiful alpine meadow filled with wild flowers for a picnic lunch.

'Sit down and rest,' he instructed, spreading out a blanket on the lush green grass. 'You still have to walk back to the chair-lift.'

'I am feeling it a bit,' Lily admitted, passing her hand over her stomach protectively, then curling her spine forwards and rubbing the small of her back.

'Let me.' Vito dropped down beside her and began to tirelessly rub the exact spot that was aching, right above the base of her spine.

'Oh, that feels good,' Lily murmured, taking a long breath and enjoying the firm, hot pressure of Vito's palm on her back. 'I wish I had the energy to walk down there,' she added, gazing across the incredible landscape to the crystal-clear mountain lake.

'I'll take you tomorrow,' Vito said. 'I know a different route that will involve less walking.'

'You're spoiling me.' Lily turned and looked at him. 'But don't you have to get back to the city?'

'Business can wait.' Vito shrugged. 'Summer will be over soon and, beautiful as this place is in winter, it's not so warm and welcoming for a picnic then.'

'I can't imagine it bleak and windswept, or covered with snow,' Lily said. 'We've had such lovely weather.'

'Let's make the most of it.' Vito opened the hamper he had carried with them, pulling out a bottle of mineral water, some chilled fruit-juice and a mouth-watering array of food that the housekeeper had prepared.

'You know, I don't think we should stay away too long,' Lily said. 'I hate to think of Giovanni with no one visiting him.'

'He has visitors,' Vito replied shortly. 'He wasn't a total recluse before you came.'

'I didn't say he was,' Lily said, upset by the sudden abruptness in Vito's tone. 'Anyway, I thought you were pleased I've been keeping your grandfather company.'

'And I thought you were happy staying here,' Vito said. 'But if you'd rather go home we'll fly back this afternoon.'

'Why does it always have to be all or nothing with you?' Lily voiced her frustration without thinking. She loved the fact that Vito was a strong, decisive man—but sometimes she wished he didn't have to see everything in black and white.

'I don't know what you mean,' he said, briskly passing her a plate of food. Lily took it glumly. Suddenly it didn't look so delicious any more.

'I mean I *have* been happy here—incredibly happy,' Lily said, watching Vito's thunderous face. 'That doesn't stop me thinking about Giovanni. But I didn't mean we have to go back immediately.'

'He has people caring for him twenty-four hours a day.' Vito took a savage bite of bread and stared at the rugged mountains across the valley.

He thought about his grandfather. He owed it to him to make his last days as happy as possible. And, although for some reason it suddenly irked him, he did know how much Giovanni counted on Lily's visits to cheer him up.

He cursed his selfishness at wanting to keep Lily away from the city for his own pleasure. There was nothing for it now. They'd have to return to Venice.

'I love your grandfather,' Lily said unexpectedly, catching his full attention. 'He accepts me and he doesn't judge me.'

'He doesn't know what you've done,' Vito said in a tightly controlled voice, wishing Lily hadn't said something to remind him of her betrayal. 'I *do* know what you've done,' he added. 'But I'm not the one who keeps bringing the subject up. I know the truth.'

'Our son won't grow up knowing his great-grandfather,' Lily said, as if she was wrapped up in her own thoughts and hadn't heard a word he'd said. 'But Giovanni wants him to grow up knowing about his family history—with a real sense of where he came from and where he belongs.'

Vito stared at her, unable to believe that she was still carrying on in the same vein. He felt a muscle start to pulse at his temple, and he clenched his fists, trying to control his rising anger. *Why* would she say things that were bound to make him remember that she had been unfaithful to him?

'I never felt I belonged. My father didn't want me, and my mother could barely cope,' she said. 'More than anything I want our son to know he's truly wanted and loved. Know he belongs with his family.'

Vito gritted his teeth, not trusting himself to speak. Why didn't she seem to care, or even realise, that she was skating on thin ice?

'My grandfather is old now,' Vito said. 'You wouldn't have found him so easy-going in his younger days. He was a formidable man.'

'Of course he was. He still is,' she responded instantly, looking at him sharply. 'It obviously runs in the family.'

'Now that he's old, he knows his time is limited,' Vito continued. 'I believe that has brought his remaining wishes into very sharp focus.'

'I agree,' Lily said. 'I thought that's what we were talking about.'

'We are talking about his desire for a grandson.'

'That's what we are giving him,' Lily said.

'That's what he *thinks* we are giving him.' Vito spoke through gritted teeth. 'The fact that for the sake of my grandfather's happiness I am prepared to publicly accept the child as my own does not mean I have forgotten the truth.'

'Nor have I,' Lily said quietly. She pushed her curly hair off her face with an exasperated gesture.

'I thought we'd got past this,' Vito said. 'The pretence that the baby is mine is for the rest of the world. Don't insult me by acting like *I* don't know the truth.'

'You don't seem to,' Lily said simply. 'And I don't know why you won't give me a chance. I agreed to your wishes not to mention it any more, because I knew there was no chance we'd ever sort things out if we kept arguing. But I thought a bond was growing between us now, and I don't understand why you keep shutting out what I'm saying.'

Vito clenched his fists and dragged in a controlled breath. No matter what he said, she just kept on claiming innocence. It was starting to grate on his nerves. He would not put up with it any more.

'I know he's not mine,' he said. 'Because I know that I can't have children.'

CHAPTER ELEVEN

LILY stared at him in shock. His expression was tightly controlled, but she could see the strain he was feeling by the lines of tension around his blue eyes. Suddenly, despite the fact she *knew* he could father a child, she realised that he really did believe that he couldn't.

'Of course you can,' she said at last. 'You are. I mean, I'm pregnant and you are the father.'

'For God's sake!' Vito exclaimed, surging to his feet and raking his fingers through his short hair. 'It's time to let that ridiculous charade go.'

She looked up at him carefully, trying to see what he was keeping hidden beneath his rigid expression. She was still sitting on the rug in the meadow and he towered over her, his white shirt and black hair outlined by the blue mountain-sky.

A light breeze tugged his fringe forwards, and he scraped it back from his face again with an impatient jerk of his hand. The gesture revealed just how tightly wound he was.

Lily got to her feet, her aching back and increased size making her feel awkward, and stood in front of him. Instinctively, she reached out a hand and placed it on his forearm. The skin was warm and supple beneath her fingers, but his muscles were as hard and immovable as steel.

'I can't let it go, because it's the truth,' Lily said simply.

She saw the change in him instantly and, despite the tight rein his was keeping on his temper, she knew he was about to explode if she didn't say something to defuse the anger that was building in him.

'Why do you think that?' she asked gently. 'Were tests done?'

Vito took a shuddering breath and turned to stare in the direction of the crystal-clear lake. Lily knew he wasn't really seeing the spectacular view. He was deep in his thoughts and memories.

'Capricia and I were unsuccessful when we tried to start a family,' he said, startling Lily with his sudden candour. 'After a time we submitted ourselves to fertility testing.' He paused for a moment, but when he continued Lily could hear the strain crackling in his voice. 'I was the one who could not have children.'

'A mistake must have been made,' Lily said automatically.

'There was no mistake,' Vito said curtly. 'Sit down and eat something. Then we'll pack up and leave.'

He pulled his mobile phone out of the back pocket of his dark jeans and pressed a speed-dial number, presumably for his assistant. Without another glance for Lily, he turned his back and walked away a few steps as he talked, effectively shutting himself off from her.

She sat down on the rug, watching him with a troubled expression. Suddenly everything that had happened was starting to make sense.

He believed that he was infertile—so when she'd become pregnant he'd assumed that she'd been unfaithful. In his mind, that was logical. He thought there was no other way she could have conceived. That explained his anger towards her—but it did *not* excuse it.

If he had told her the truth that Easter weekend, she would have tried to reason with him, persuade him that there'd been a mistake. He could have had the results of his fertility tests double-checked. Obviously there must have been a mix up. Or maybe something had changed. She wasn't an expert on fertility, but she *knew* that she was pregnant, and that he was the *only* one who could be the father.

She looked at him talking on his phone. Standing there with the awe-inspiring backdrop of the Dolomite mountains behind him, he looked as magnificent as the noble terrain. But he was also as cold and uncompromising as those harsh, jagged peaks that soared above the verdant valleys.

She understood that his belief that he could not have children must have hurt him—especially when he was the last surviving man in his proud Italian family. But he had hurt her—throwing her out onto the street when she had done nothing wrong, and then coercing her into a marriage that he'd never meant to be permanent.

He should have told her the truth. Instead he'd misled her—first making her believe she was responsible for birth control that in reality he thought was unnecessary. Then making vicious accusations when she had never, ever given him any reason to doubt her. Then finally, worst of all, he had shamelessly used his knowledge of her troubled childhood to manipulate her.

Suddenly a wave of anger rose up out of nowhere, startling her with its intensity. He'd trusted a medical report over the woman he had shared his life with. He'd never given her a chance.

She stared up at him balefully. He had treated her appallingly, and she had let him get away with it. Well, not any more.

At last he finished his conversation with his assistant, slid his phone back into his pocket and sat down on the rug.

'You haven't eaten,' he said, finally looking at her again.

As she met his gaze a crackle of energy passed between them.

His eyes widened in surprise, and she knew he had recognised the anger that was building inside her.

'When we get back you must have the fertility tests repeated.' The sound of her own voice thrumming with intensity startled her. But she continued to stare him down, determined to make him see that she meant business.

'Why would I subject myself to that humiliation again?' Vito bit out, the planes of his face tightening as he spoke. 'In the circumstances, don't you think it would be better to let sleeping dogs lie? Or are you simply masochistic enough to want incontrovertible proof of your infidelity?'

'I want proof of my innocence!' Lily snapped. 'And, if you won't have those tests repeated, I'll get a DNA test after the baby is born.'

'Are you mad?' Vito demanded. 'If I won't submit to a fertility test, what makes you think I'll be party to a DNA test?'

'I'll go to Giovanni,' Lily declared. 'His DNA will prove a family connection.'

Vito cursed violently in Italian and surged to his feet, hauling her up by her arms.

'You go too far!' His words throbbed with barely contained fury, and suddenly Lily felt herself quaking under the sheer force of his rage. Of course she'd never do anything to hurt Giovanni, but Vito's refusal to listen to reason was driving her to distraction.

Then, with one powerful arm around her waist and one hand gripping her upper arm, he started marching her away, back in the direction of the chair-lift.

Everywhere they made contact she could feel Vito's thunderous energy burning into her body. It felt like she was caught up in an escalating storm, still waiting in trepidation for it to reach its maximum force.

In barely any time they reached the main footpath, and Vito eased his grip slightly as two young male hikers approached them. He hailed them in English, then quickly switched to fluent German as he identified their nationality.

Lily couldn't catch everything he was saying, but, as he thrust a wad of euros their way and pointed back to the abandoned picnic-hamper in the meadow, she understood what had just transpired. Vito was so used to issuing orders and being obeyed that apparently he'd thought nothing of paying the young men to clear away their mess.

She didn't have time to ponder what it must be like to be Vito—so powerful and self-assured that he expected complete strangers to jump to do his bidding— because at that moment he continued walking her briskly towards the chair-lift.

They flew back to Venice in virtual silence, and the days that followed were miserable for Lily. Refusing point-blank to engage in conversation with her, Vito kept well away. He left for work early, returned late at night, and only spoke to her when absolutely necessary.

She felt like she was trapped in a nightmare, and

there was no escape that she could see. At first she thought she must leave Venice—but it wasn't that simple. It wasn't just the gnawing ache that filled her soul at the thought of leaving Vito, there were other things to consider.

Her pregnancy was too advanced for it to be easy to travel, and the idea of arriving in London with a baby due to arrive so soon was frankly terrifying. At least here in Venice she was already under medical care.

And the other thought that kept plaguing her was how devastated Giovanni would be. She knew the baby *was* his true great-grandson—but if she left she didn't know what Vito would tell him. Although she still felt horribly betrayed by how Vito had used her, she shared his desire to make his grandfather happy. So she'd have to wait for the baby to come before she could do anything.

As the days went by, the anger she'd felt towards Vito in the alpine meadow slowly ebbed away, and she was left feeling dejected and lonely.

Time seemed to drag on interminably, sometimes making it feel like she was going to be pregnant for ever. She still had more than a month to go, and she honestly didn't know how she was going to get through it.

She visited Giovanni every morning, travelling on the canals both ways, and in the afternoons she took refuge in her supply of paperback books. She slept a lot. And, in between sleeping, reading and visiting Giovanni, she sat in the baby's nursery, trying not to think about the implications of Vito's stunning revelation that he believed himself to be infertile.

At first it had been like a light switching on in her mind, because it finally explained why he'd assumed she'd been unfaithful. Then she had felt anger at his lack of trust in her. Now she felt something different.

Unwanted.

If Vito hadn't believed himself infertile, *he would never have married her.*

Right from the start she had understood that Vito wasn't interested in a serious commitment to her. At the time it hadn't mattered to her. She'd been overwhelmed just by being with him, and had assumed his 'no commitment' rule was not a reflection of what he thought about her but simply a rule he lived by.

Now she knew differently. It *had been* about her.

She'd been good enough to be his lover, but not good enough to be his wife. Not until he'd seen an opportunity for her to give him, for his aging grandfather, something he thought he couldn't get anywhere else.

And even then it had taken the time pressure of his grandfather's failing health to bring him to his decision. She couldn't forget that when she'd got pregnant he had ruthlessly thrown her out of his life without a second thought.

But, after they were married, she had realised that she loved him. She had clung to the hope that maybe, if she managed to convince him that she had never been unfaithful, he would start to open his heart to her. She had to believe that there was something between them, a tiny little ember that could be brought to life in the right circumstances.

However, now she knew he believed himself to be infertile, all hope seemed to be gone. It really was only circumstance that had prompted him to marry her. Once he discovered he was not infertile there would be nothing tying him to her any more. He could have any woman he wanted.

* * *

'You look tired,' Giovanni said, taking his spectacles off and laying them down with his Venetian newspaper beside him on his large bed.

'A little,' Lily admitted, easing herself down into the comfy chair Giovanni kept near his bed especially for her visits. 'I don't know why. I'm not doing much these days.'

'What do you mean?' he exclaimed. 'You are growing my grandson inside your body—that is something!'

Lily smiled. Her visits to Giovanni always lifted her spirits.

'Not long now, and you'll get to meet him,' she said, hoping that it was true. The doctors had been pleased with how stable Giovanni's health had been lately, but he was still a very frail old man.

'I won't watch him grow up,' he said. 'But I'm not going anywhere until I've seen him with my own eyes.'

Suddenly Lily felt tears welling up. She blinked them away, feeling self-conscious, but Giovanni hadn't noticed. He was gazing forward with a smile on his face.

'I promise I'll teach him everything you told me about your life and Venice,' she said, keeping her voice steady with a determined effort.

'You've made me a very happy old man,' Giovanni said, turning to look at her. 'Only the very lucky can live long enough to see their great-grandchildren. I don't know if I've ever told you how pleased I am that *you* are to be the mother.'

'Thank you. You've always been so good to me,' Lily replied, hearing her voice tremble with heartfelt emotion.

'You were worth the wait,' he said with a lively smile. 'You know, after Capricia, I was worried my grandson might not have good taste in women.'

'Really?' Lily asked, her curiosity piqued even though she knew it was potentially a controversial subject. 'But if they'd stayed together, and if they'd started a family, you would have had longer to get to know your grandchildren.'

'Capricia's children?' Giovanni said in disgust. 'I never understood why he married her. She might have been Venetian, but she was not a good wife for him. And I doubt that she would have agreed to motherhood for a long time.'

'What do you mean?' Despite her better judgement telling her to keep off the subject of Vito's first wife, Lily wanted to know more.

'She was far too busy living it up—enjoying her selfish existence, spending his money on frivolous things,' Giovanni said. 'She's still the same, except now she's in Rio de Janeiro spending her Brazilian lover's money—if what my contacts tell me is true.'

'Contacts?' Lily smiled, trying to appear lighthearted even though her heart felt anything but light.

'What do you think?' Giovanni sounded affronted. 'Just because I'm old and in bed I know nothing?'

'Of course not,' Lily laughed, but she couldn't help wondering what he knew about her and Vito.

'But don't think about Capricia,' Giovanni added. 'Vito never loved her the way he loves you. Anyone can see you two are soulmates—like me and my dear Anna Maria.'

Lily forced a smile and looked down at her hands clasped in her lap, feeling heartsick. She knew now that Vito had never loved her at all.

'I nearly forgot—I have a surprise for you,' Giovanni said.

'A surprise?' Lily repeated, pleased at the distraction. She didn't want to bring Giovanni down by looking dejected. But she hoped he wasn't going to make things awkward for her with Vito by giving her any more family heirlooms. She loved the antique necklace he'd given her the first day, but she hadn't seen it since Vito had taken it away from her.

'Yes. Talking of my Anna Maria reminded me...' He smiled, and Lily knew from his dreamy expression he was still thinking of his wife. 'I remembered her favourite thing when she was pregnant, and I thought you might like it too.'

Lily smiled expectantly, intrigued to get another glimpse of the woman who had so clearly captured Giovanni's heart.

'I can't come with you to see how you like it,' he said, pressing a button to call a member of his staff. 'But you must tell me when you visit tomorrow.'

At that moment his housekeeper came into the room and he told her to show Lily to her surprise. From the way she responded to the instruction, she had obviously been involved in the arrangements, and as Giovanni settled down for a nap she led Lily away to a part of the *palazzo* she had never seen before.

Down two flights of stairs, across an absolutely delightful courtyard complete with citrus trees in giant terracotta pots, and in through another double door, Lily found herself gazing at the most inviting thing she had seen for days.

A cool, blue swimming-pool.

'Oh my!' she sighed, suddenly aching to ease her tired body into the water.

The housekeeper explained how Giovanni had had the pool repaired and refilled, showed her where the changing and showering facilities were, and finally presented her with a collection of maternity swimwear.

Just minutes later Lily was floating on her back in

the blissfully cool and supportive water. She rolled over and slowly swam a length of the pool, admiring the detailed mosaics beneath the rippling water.

She loved Giovanni for this gift to her. It was absolutely perfect in every way.

Suddenly tears sprung unchecked to her eyes.

Vito's grandfather had shown her unstinting kindness like no one in her life ever had before. He treated her with respect and as an individual he genuinely wanted to get to know. Her own father had never done that. He didn't even want to know her at all.

And now Vito, her husband, didn't seem to want to know her either.

Vito strode through the narrow Venetian streets impatiently. It was late afternoon, and he'd come home from the office early for the third day in a row only to find Lily was not at the *palazzo*. Since they'd returned from the mountains, she'd started spending more and more time at *Ca' Salvatore*. In fact she was rarely at home these days, and it was beginning to bother him.

He knew that his grandfather had refilled his swimming pool for her, which he acknowledged was a very thoughtful gesture. And apparently Lily loved swimming—which was something he hadn't known about her. But surely she couldn't be spending *all* day in the pool?

Suddenly the memory of their conversation in the meadow loomed large and uncomfortable in his mind. He swore under his breath, cursing himself for telling her about his infertility. Things had been progressing smoothly between them up until that point, and he wished he hadn't chosen that moment to upset the balance of their relationship.

He didn't understand what had driven him to come clean, but blamed it on Lily. He'd spent so much time alone with her that she had whittled her way through his defences. He had quite simply let his guard down. He wouldn't make that mistake again. He shouldn't have made it this time.

He remembered all too well the scornful look on Capricia's face when she'd waved the doctor's report stating his infertility under his nose. It was unbelievable that he'd been foolish enough to put himself through the same humiliation twice.

He'd been young and naive when he'd married Capricia, hoping that she would be the perfect Venetian wife to bring up the next generation of Salvatores. It hadn't worked out that way. But he'd thought he had learnt something from the experience—to protect his pride if nothing else.

His infertility had driven a wedge into his first marriage. To alleviate her disappointment in his failure, Capricia had thrown herself into a wild life of socialising and travel. They'd grown apart, but he hadn't made any effort to hold onto their marriage. When Capricia had finally left, he'd been pleased. With her gone there should have been no reminder of his shame.

But, no matter how hard he'd tried, he hadn't been able to forget what had happened. He was accustomed to success, and his failure as a man continued to burn into him mercilessly.

Dealing with the unrelenting sense of humiliation was the hardest challenge he had ever faced. So he'd vowed never to let a serious relationship compromise his defences again. He could not father a child—therefore there was no point in long-term commitment.

It was only his grandfather's dying wish that had made him reassess his decision, and that had led him to marry Lily.

Lily was not like Capricia—she hadn't responded with scorn when she'd discovered he was infertile. But the shock of the news had made her show her true colours. And the way she was acting now told him what she really thought of him.

He knew he'd knocked the ground out from under her. She was no longer able to cling to her story that she hadn't been unfaithful. She'd seemed stunned at first, but that had been quickly followed by anger—presumably because he'd made her look a fool.

But, whatever her feelings, it was part of their agreement that she kept them to herself. He didn't appreciate the message she was sending his household by spending all her time at *Ca' Salvatore*. In the daytime it was fine—but not in the evening when he was expected home from work.

He was still deep in thought as he strode into the old courtyard at *Ca' Salvatore*. Lily was sleeping on a recliner under the protection of the cloistered passage that led to the entrance to the pool.

He stopped and gazed at her. She looked beautiful— utterly enchanting, but also achingly vulnerable. She was turned slightly on her side, with her silken hair spread out behind her like an angel's wings, and her arms were folded protectively over her stomach.

As he gazed at her, all the bad feelings that had built up during his walk from the *palazzo* melted away. How could he feel angry when presented with a vision of such celestial beauty?

He had missed her—had missed the time they'd spent together.

He sat down beside her on another chair, suddenly content to wait until she awoke naturally. She must have only been dozing, because she started to stir almost immediately.

'*Ciao,*' he said, reaching out to tuck a blonde curl which had fallen forward behind her ear. 'I thought I'd find you here.'

'How long have you been sitting there?' Lily asked, groggily pushing herself upright.

'Not long. In fact I just arrived,' Vito said, twisting on his chair to glance around. 'You know, it's years since I was in this courtyard. I used to play football here.'

'Really?' she said, looking at the citrus trees in terracotta pots and the curved marble benches arranged around the trickling fountain-pool in the centre. 'There's a lot of obstacles.'

'Good for my dribbling skills.' Vito smiled as he remembered. 'There's nothing like getting tackled by marble bench—it gets you right in the shins.'

Lily blinked and rubbed her eyes, still feeling half asleep.

Why was he being so nice all of a sudden? His smile completely changed his face, erasing the vertical crease that had been gouged between his eyes in the weeks since they'd returned from the mountains.

'There's a lot of windows too,' she added, trying to ignore the way his smile tugged at her heart. She couldn't let herself start to fall for him all over again every time he decided to turn on the charm.

'Yes—I smashed quite a few of them,' Vito said. 'The housekeeper covered it up at first, but when my grandfather found out he certainly took me to task.'

Lily gazed at him, trying to imagine what he might

have looked like as a boy. For the housekeeper to have covered up broken windows he must have been quite a charmer, even back then. She wondered if he had photos. It would be intriguing to get some idea what their son might look like.

An unpleasantly cold feeling washed over her. Vito wouldn't show her photos because he was still denying the possibility that he could be the father. She slumped back on the recliner, suddenly feeling weary and washed out.

'Are you all right?' Vito's voice sounded genuinely concerned.

'I'm fine. Just tired.' She picked up her glass of water, deliberately not letting herself look at his face. She knew his expression would reflect what she had just heard in his voice. If she saw that concern, combined with his heart-stoppingly good looks, she knew her defences would start to melt.

'You look sad.' Vito reached out to touch her arm, and the gesture of comfort sent a wave of warmth through her which was at odds with what her brain was telling her. 'Why are you unhappy?'

'Because you only married me for the baby inside me,' she said, the honest words coming out as a reaction to the conflict she was feeling inside.

'You knew that—I told you that from the start.' Vito let his hand drop from her arm abruptly. 'Why is that an issue now? Are you saying that you thought there was another reason?'

'I thought—I hoped—there was *something* between us, more than just the child inside me that you still refuse to even consider is yours.' She put her feet down onto the marble flagstones, looking beside the recliner to locate her flat sandals. 'Now I know I was wrong. All I am to you is a convenient baby-machine.'

She rammed her feet into her sandals and pushed herself quickly to her feet.

Suddenly she felt a strange sensation inside her, followed by a gush of warm fluid down her legs. She stared down at the puddle on the ground in a moment's bewilderment. The baby wasn't due for another month. Then she heard Vito's voice, strong and reassuring.

'Your water just broke,' he said, sweeping her up into his arms and striding swiftly to the *palazzo's* water entrance. 'We're going straight to hospital.'

CHAPTER TWELVE

LILY stared in awe at the baby sleeping in her arms. He was utterly beautiful. Her heart ached with how small and perfect he was, and she didn't think she'd ever be able to take her eyes off him again.

He had arrived so suddenly. By the time they'd reached the hospital her labour had already been well advanced. But everything had gone smoothly and he'd been born at nine-thirty in the evening, weighing a healthy six pounds.

Vito had been amazing during the labour and delivery, an absolute tower of strength and encouragement. He had known exactly when to hold her or rub her back, or whisper fortifying words of comfort in her ear. He had never left her side for a moment—until now, when she'd had to urge him to go and call his grandfather.

The door of her private room opened and she looked up, expecting to see Vito returning. But instead it was the doctor.

'I gather the baby has already fed a little,' the doctor said. 'That's good. He's a strong little fellow for his size. But I'm afraid I must disturb him to take a small sample of his blood.'

'What for?' Lily asked, assuming it was some kind

of routine test done for all babies. 'Why do you have to do it now while he's asleep?'

'I think it best to find out whether he has inherited his father's rare blood-type as soon as possible,' the doctor replied, talking as if he thought Lily knew what he was referring to. 'Being delivered at thirty-six weeks we wouldn't expect any problems,' he continued. 'But in the circumstances it's prudent to know the facts regarding his blood type.'

'I don't understand what you are talking about,' Lily said, hugging the tiny baby protectively to her. At that moment Vito returned and she stared up at him, a wave of panic rising up within her.

'I was just explaining about the situation with your blood type,' the doctor said to Vito as he crossed to Lily's side.

'You didn't *explain*.' Lily flashed her gaze anxiously between the two men. 'You just told me we needed to find it out, in case something went wrong!'

'Just a precaution,' the doctor said, pulling up a chair next to her and placing the equipment he needed to draw a blood sample on a small tray on the table beside them.

'Why didn't you tell me about this?' Lily looked up at Vito accusingly, still keeping her baby out of the doctor's reach.

He stood as straight as a ramrod with an unreadable expression on his face, but Lily knew the answer to her question. He hadn't told her because he'd thought it was irrelevant—he didn't believe the baby was his.

'I'm sure he just didn't want to worry you,' the doctor said. 'It's extremely unlikely that the baby will have inherited it.'

'What if he has?' Lily asked, fear ripping through her.

'Well, as you are obviously aware, your husband is as strong as an ox. It only becomes an issue if he needs a blood transfusion.'

'What happens then?' Lily pressed.

'It's harder to find suitable donor-blood. That's why we want to be prepared, so we don't have any surprises at a time we could do without them.' He reached up gently to ease the blanket away from the infant. 'If you can hold him steady, we'll get this over with as painlessly as possible.'

'But what if you can't find the right blood to give him?' Lily asked, feeling increasingly anxious. It all sounded very complicated and worrying.

'There's no reason at all to think we'll *need* blood for a transfusion,' the doctor said firmly. 'But, if for some reason we do, then of course we'll find it. It's just that we may have to search further afield.'

Lily took a deep breath and lowered the baby unto her lap. She unwrapped the blanket so that the doctor could take the blood sample.

As the needle pricked his fragile skin he opened his eyes in horrified protest. A moment later he opened his mouth and started crying.

Lily felt her lower lip start to tremble in response, and she hugged her son close to her. It was unbearable to see her baby upset.

'I'll get this sample off to the lab,' the doctor said, taking his leave.

'Lily…I…' Vito was standing close to her, but she didn't look up. For the first time ever, she thought he sounded uncertain—but right then all her attention was on her newborn baby.

'Leave me alone,' she said, feeling like she had been punched in the stomach.

She unbuttoned her nightdress and tried to offer the baby up to her breast. But the position wasn't right, and after a frantic moment of silence as he rooted unsuccessfully for her nipple he started crying again.

Without a saying a word, Vito dropped down on his knees in front of them. He cupped the baby's head gently and guided it forward to Lily's breast. Just as the baby opened his mouth as wide as possible to let out a mewling cry, Vito nudged his head forward and he latched onto the nipple successfully.

Lily looked down at her baby suckling contentedly, and took care to keep his position steady. Vito had rocked back on his heels, but his eyes were still locked on the infant.

'I asked you to leave me alone,' she said quietly, lifting her eyes to meet his. Vito's gaze was troubled, but she was too angry with him to give it any thought.

'But—'

'I don't want you here,' she said, hearing her own voice crackle with ice. 'Your pride has made you selfish. I can't believe that you were so arrogant and stubborn that you let your lack of trust in me make you ignore something that could affect our baby's wellbeing.'

Vito paced up and down his study, looking repeatedly at his fax machine, waiting for it to whir into action.

He'd had a miserable night. The worst night of his life—even harder than when he'd forced Lily to leave Venice back in March. That night he'd been upset, but he'd focussed his anger on what he'd thought of as her betrayal. He hadn't been forced to look in the mirror at his own decisions and actions.

Now, everything was different. His personal demons

were howling round the room with him, unrelenting in their attack on his well-built defences.

What if he'd been wrong?

Wrong about everything?

The thought plagued him, constantly looming up in his mind. He tried to reject it, the way he'd always successfully rejected Lily's claims. But now it seemed as if she was finally getting through to him.

What if he really was the father of the baby?

The look of fear on her face when she hadn't understood what the doctor was saying about his rare blood-group haunted him. And the cold look of disgust on her face when she'd thrown him out of her hospital room stabbed into him like a jagged blade.

Suddenly the fax machine came to life. He was rooted to the spot, watching as the sheet of white paper curled out.

A copy of his fertility-test results.

All those years ago he'd never read them for himself. The disdainful look on Capricia's face had seen to that. His pride hadn't been able to stand it. Even providing the sample in the first place, letting his virility be put to the test, had been hard to bear. He'd never considered getting a physical examination or second opinion. The brutal assault on his masculine pride had been unendurable.

He reached for the fax and hesitated, blood pounding in his temples.

He was terrified at what he would read.

Would the results show that he had been right all along, make him relive his humiliation yet again? Or would he find out that Lily had been telling the truth—that he was guilty of treating her appallingly when she didn't deserve it? And that her beautiful baby boy was his son?

He picked up the document and looked at it.

His heart thudded in his chest and his palms were suddenly damp with sweat.

Results: every likelihood of excellent fertility at this time.

Lily lay on her side in the hospital bed watching her newborn baby sleeping in his crib. The nurses had made her put him down, told her that if she didn't sleep when he did she'd become exhausted and her milk wouldn't flow. But, even though she'd been awake all night, sleep would not come.

Vito had left when she'd asked and he'd never returned.

She didn't know what she had expected—she hadn't exactly been thinking straight at the time. But despite the fact he had proven once again just how little faith he had in her, she wished he were there with her.

She couldn't stop thinking about how wonderful he'd been during the birth. She couldn't have asked for more. It must mean something. Maybe, although love was not part of the equation for him, he did care about her a little.

But now she had sent him away.

She squeezed her eyes shut, wishing sleep would come and ease her misery. But then she heard a quiet sound and, although it could have been a nurse returning to check up on her and the baby, she knew it was Vito.

She rolled over and tried to sit up, but after the rigours of the birth she was stiff and sore. Vito was by her side in a second, gently helping her into a comfortable position.

'Thank you.' She looked up at him standing beside the bed, and her eyes widened with surprise as she took in his appearance. He'd showered and shaved since last night, but his face was ashen and painfully troubled.

'I'm sorry.' His voice was deep and rough, as if it had been difficult for him to say that word. Or maybe it was because he was so tired. But, whatever the case, his expression was contrite as he gazed down at her on the bed.

'What for?' she asked simply.

'For everything,' he said. 'For the way I've treated you. For not trusting you. For making you marry me even though I didn't mean it to last.'

'Do you believe me now?' Lily asked, looking at the lines of stress etched around his eyes.

'Yes,' Vito said. 'I got Capricia's doctor out of bed at an ungodly hour this morning, and had him go straight to his office to fax me a copy of the results of my fertility test.'

'I don't understand,' Lily said, ignoring the wave of sadness that washed over her as she realised it wasn't anything *she* had said or done that had convinced Vito. It had taken Capricia's doctor. 'How did that make any difference? You saw those results years ago.'

'I never read them myself,' Vito admitted.

Lily stared at him in frank disbelief, too startled to mask her reaction. For a moment he actually appeared to wince with embarrassment.

'You never read them?' she gasped. 'Surely you followed up the result—repeated the test or got a second opinion?'

'No.' Vito hung his head for a moment, then took a deep breath and looked her in the eye to continue. 'I was devastated. All my dreams of becoming a father, of continuing the Salvatore line, were shattered. It seemed like an assault on my very existence.'

'Why did she do it?' Lily asked. 'What would make Capricia lie to you like that?'

'I don't know,' Vito said. 'I've been wracking my brain all night, trying to work it out. The only solution I have is that she didn't want children. I knew she didn't want to come off the Pill—but I thought I'd persuaded her to try to start a family. Presumably she just carried on taking the Pill all along.'

'I think you're right.' Lily thought about how Giovanni had described Vito's first wife. It was ironic that the old man had got her measure better than Vito. 'It must be painful to realise that the woman you loved tricked you like that.'

'I don't know if "painful" is the correct word,' Vito said. 'I'm furious with her. Furious that what she did led me to hurt you so badly.'

'You should have read the results yourself,' Lily muttered. She knew it was harsh to point that out. But she couldn't help noticing Vito had not denied loving Capricia—a woman who had deceived and cheated him. For some reason that really hurt.

'I'm sorry,' Vito said again. 'I've treated you unforgivably.'

Lily gazed at him sadly, swallowing against a hard lump in her throat. She ought to accept his apology. He was the victim of a wicked deception. If Capricia hadn't lied to him, he would never have treated *her* so badly.

But none of it was her fault. The only thing she'd ever done wrong was fall in love with Vito.

'Nothing's changed in the way I feel,' Lily said miserably. 'You never trusted me—you had to get Capricia's doctor to send you proof.'

'Something did change yesterday. I saw your fear when the doctor took the blood sample.' Vito sucked in a deep, shuddering breath and raked his hands roughly through his black hair. 'I spent the night in an agony of confusion. Once I'd admitted the possibility that you might be telling the truth, I was desperate for that to be the case. But, after Capricia left, I spent so long denying my feelings that it was almost impossible to get out of that rut. The security of encasing your deeper feelings in a layer of cold rock is hard to give up.'

His heartfelt outburst tugged at Lily's sympathies, but it was a cruel kind of torture to listen to him describing how he'd battened down his emotions after Capricia had left.

'You must have loved her very much,' she said.

'Capricia?' Vito looked at Lily in surprise.

Her hazel eyes were wide in her pale face, and the dark shadows of fatigue around them accentuated their size. She looked so small and vulnerable, sitting there in the white hospital bed, that his chest contracted painfully.

'I don't think I ever loved Capricia,' he said. 'Not really.'

'Then why did you marry her?' Lily asked.

'I was young,' Vito said. 'She was beautiful. Venetian. And at the time I foolishly thought she'd make a good wife and mother.'

Lily didn't reply, but he could see in her face what she thought of his judgement. It was terrible. It had always been terrible. In business it seemed he could do no wrong. But, in his personal life, *everything* he'd done was wrong.

Until one day, in a moment of good fortune, he'd met Lily. And then he had set about ruining that too.

'I'm sorry. I've ruined everything,' he said. 'It wasn't necessary to force you into this. I've married you when I didn't need to.'

Suddenly he saw her eyes fill with tears. As the liquid

pooled and spilled down her cheeks it felt as if someone had ripped his heart from his chest.

'Don't cry,' he said, sitting on the edge of the bed and taking her hands in his. They felt pitifully cold in his grip. 'I know we are married—but I don't see how I can hold you to that now.'

'But what about your grandfather?' she said, her voice uneven with the sound of crying.

Vito held her hands, gently warming them between his palms. Then suddenly he realised something.

Lily was more important than his grandfather.

His desire to see Giovanni end his days in contentment was still powerful. But not at the expense of Lily's happiness.

'My grandfather doesn't need to know,' Vito said carefully. 'You've given him the heir he desired. And, with your friendship, so much more than that. I can't ask you to give up your life.'

He looked at her sad face, his heart contracting painfully at her distress, and suddenly all he wanted was to take away her sadness.

'Don't cry,' he said again, leaning forward to kiss away the salty tears that were streaming down her cheeks. 'You're tired. It will seem better later. We'll work things out.'

'How *can* we work things out?' she sobbed. 'You don't need me any more. You never needed me.'

'Of course I need you!' Vito exclaimed. 'I've always needed you. From the very first time we talked I knew I had to make you part of my life.'

He cupped her face and looked at her puzzled expression. She'd stopped crying and was looking at him in confusion.

At that moment it hit him.

Like a punch in the solar plexus, he suddenly knew the truth.

He loved her.

He'd *always* loved her. That was why her pregnancy had hurt him so deeply, why he'd forced her to marry him, and why the thought of letting her go now was grinding into him like a steel bar.

He let his breath out with a whoosh, and smiled at her.

Love. That must be causing this ground-rush of emotions that was rising up to meet him as the clouds of doubt fell away, finally revealing the woman he loved.

'What?' she whispered, looking anxiously into his face. 'What is it?'

'I love you,' he said.

'But…' Lily stared at him in disbelief. Where had that suddenly come from? A moment ago he'd said he planned to divorce her—which she'd expected, now he had finally accepted he was not infertile.

So why had he said he loved her? Had she even heard correctly?

'I love you!' he said, hauling her into his arms and nearly crushing her with his exuberance. 'Oh, my God! Why have I only just realised it?'

'It can't be true,' Lily said. She couldn't let her hopes be raised. It must be guilt for what he'd put her through making him momentarily lose his common sense.

'It *is* true,' Vito said, cupping her face with gentle hands again and looking deeply into her eyes. 'I've never said anything more true in my life.'

'But…' Lily didn't know what to say. She looked deep into his sky-blue eyes, trying to suppress the tingle of excitement that was bubbling inside her. It was what she'd yearned to hear for such a long time that she hardly dared to believe it. 'Why are you saying this now?'

'I only just realised,' Vito said. 'I think I was so closed off to my feelings that it took me a long time to realise the truth. Even though it was staring me in the face all the time.'

'What do you mean?' Lily asked.

'Back before Easter, when you went to the doctor with your stomach bug,' Vito said. 'I was so worried about you.'

'I remember you waiting for me,' Lily said, thinking about the black cashmere sweater she had tossed into the canal.

'You came home looking white as a sheet, and I thought something might be seriously wrong with you.' Vito took a breath. 'I couldn't bear that thought. It cut me like knife.'

'I didn't know that,' Lily said. 'But I remember how kind you were to me. Until…'

'Until I lost my mind with jealousy,' Vito said. 'I couldn't bear the thought of you with another man. I think I lost my reason for a while.'

Lily gazed at him, the lines of his distress clearly etched onto his face.

'It's all right,' she said. 'It turned out all right.'

'Thank God for Luigi,' Vito said. 'And for your friend Anna.'

'I would have been okay,' she said. 'I don't need someone to look after me.'

'I know,' he said seriously. 'You are the strongest person I know. When I think how you dealt with all the appalling difficulties I threw your way… I'm sorry.'

'Please, stop saying that,' Lily said, placing the flat of her palm against his chest. She could feel his heart beating beneath her hand, and the power of its rhythm gave her hope. 'We can't turn back the clock. Let's go forwards.'

'Will you stay with me?' Vito asked. 'Give me another chance?'

'Of course I will,' Lily said, feeling tears of happiness start to well up in her eyes.

'Why are you crying?' Vito leant forward to brush his thumb across her damp cheek.

'Because I love you too,' Lily answered. 'I've always loved you.'

A smile of incredulous happiness broke across Vito's face. Then the next moment he was crushing her in his arms again.

'I can't believe it.' Vito's voice was muffled against her hair. 'Last night I was despairing that things could ever be right—and now all my dreams have come true.'

His words reflected exactly how Lily was feeling, and she clung to him tightly, feeling like she'd never let go again. But a moment later a tiny, mewling cry from the cot interrupted them.

'He's awake!' Vito's voice was full of love and pride, as if waking up was the cleverest thing any baby had ever done.

'Would you like to pick him up?' Lily watched as Vito lifted the baby out of the cot. His gentle hands seemed almost as big as his son as he gazed down at the crumpled, newborn face with adoring eyes.

'What does he need?' Vito turned to her for advice.

'I don't know,' she replied honestly. 'I'm new at this. Perhaps I should try to feed him.' She unfastened the top few buttons of her nightdress and held out her hands for the baby. Vito placed him gently in her arms, then doing the same as the previous evening, guided the little head towards her nipple.

'Ah, that's the idea. I like to see a little bit of teamwork.' Lily recognised the doctor's voice and lifted her gaze to see him walking into the room. 'We have the results of the blood test,' he continued. 'Unfortunately it seems this little fellow is following in your footsteps with a rare blood-type.'

Lily looked at Vito's face to see how he would respond to this physical proof that he was the baby's father. To her surprise a worried frown marred his features.

'That's a blow,' he said. 'I was hoping he would have taken after his mother.'

'There's nothing to worry about,' the doctor said. 'Your wife and I talked some more last night, and she understands now that it won't be a problem. It's just something it pays to be aware of.'

He walked over to the bed and gave a satisfied nod as he saw how well the baby was feeding. 'I'll be back to check on you later,' he said as he left them alone again.

'I thought you'd be pleased,' Lily said. 'Pleased to have concrete proof of your paternity.'

'I didn't need it.' He turned and held her gaze with serious eyes. 'I have all the proof I need, in here,' he said, placing his hand over his heart.

Lily felt her lips quiver again as once more her eyes filled with tears of happiness.

'I love you,' she said.

'And I you,' Vito replied. 'With all of my heart and soul.'

EPILOGUE

'MY GREAT-GRANDSON,' Giovanni breathed, looking down at the little baby cradled carefully in his arms.

Lily sat next to him on his huge bed, feeling tears well up in her own eyes as she heard the tremulous notes of awe and gratitude in his voice.

'He's called Giovanni,' she said.

The old man lifted his head to stare at her with sparkling blue eyes, momentarily speechless as the information sunk in.

'Thank you,' he said. 'Thank you for making me very happy.'

'It's an honour to do so,' Lily said, leaning forward to kiss his paper-thin cheek. 'I can never explain what your kindness has meant to me. How delighted I am to be part of your family, and how much pleasure I have knowing that my son will carry on your family name.'

'You are wearing the necklace,' he said, suddenly noticing the exquisite piece of antique jewellery that was fastened round Lily's neck. 'When you never wore it I thought it was not to your taste after all.'

'Oh no, I love it,' Lily said, reaching up to trail her fingertips over the smooth beads. 'Vito was having it checked by antique jewellery experts to make sure it was strong enough to wear. I didn't want to damage it.'

'But today is an important occasion, *Nonno*—introducing you to my son,' Vito said, gazing at his wife. She was the most beautiful thing he'd ever seen, and just looking at her made his heart swell with the great love he felt for her.

He was embarrassed that he'd kept hold of the necklace for months after it had been restored, but somehow he had never been able to find the right time to return it to her. But then she had asked for it this morning, smoothing away his awkwardness with tender kisses, and making him fall in love with her all over again for her kindness and understanding.

'Yes, it is,' Giovanni said, his eyes focussed back on the baby again, but Vito could tell he was beginning to grow weary.

'We'll leave you to rest now, *Nonno*.' He lifted the baby gently out of his grandfather's arms. 'Don't worry—we'll come back tomorrow.'

'See that you do,' Giovanni said, but the abruptness of his words was softened by the fact that his eyes were already starting to close as he leant his head back against his pillows.

Vito led the way down to the canal entrance of *Ca' Salvatore* and, once Lily was safely on the boat, he passed baby Giovanni down to her.

'You've made my grandfather very happy,' Vito said as he stepped down into the boat and sat next to her. A thick autumn fog was rolling in from the Adriatic, and the city was taking on an eerie quality. It made him want to hurry home and snuggle his little family up, safe and warm inside.

'I meant what I said to him.' Lily looked up through

the fog at the magnificent façade of the baroque *palazzo* as the boat started to move out into the flow of traffic on the Grand Canal. 'About being proud that my son will be part of this family.'

She dropped her gaze to look into the gorgeous face of the man she adored, and as their eyes met a little frisson of pleasure ran through her. She was tired from looking after their newborn baby, but she had never felt so happy in her entire life.

'I love you. And I am so proud to have you as my wife,' Vito said, slipping his arm around her and hugging her gently. 'You belong here in Venice. You belong with me.'

'I love it here,' Lily said as the boat turned off the Grand Canal to head towards home. Tendrils of fog were creeping into the smaller waterways, and the boat driver was taking it carefully. 'But, more than that, I love *you*. And I'll always belong with you.'

Lucy Monroe

*delivers two more books from
her irresistible Royal Brides series.*

Billionaire businessman Sebastian Hawk and
Sheikh Amir are bound by one woman: Princess Lina.
Sebastian has been hired to protect Lina—but all he
wants to do is make her his. Amir has arranged to marry
her—but it's his virgin secretary he wants in his bed!

Two men driven by desire—who will they
make their brides?

FORBIDDEN: THE BILLIONAIRE'S VIRGIN PRINCESS

Sebastian Hawk is strong, passionate
and will do anything to claim the woman
he wants. Only, Lina is forbidden to him
and promised to another man....

Available July 2008

Don't miss
HIRED: THE SHEIKH'S SECRETARY MISTRESS

On sale August 2008

HP12739

HARLEQUIN *Presents*

EXTRA

THE BOSS'S MISTRESS

Out of the office…and into his bed

These ruthless, powerful men are used
to having their own way in the office—
and with their mistresses they're also
boss in the bedroom!

**Don't miss any of our fantastic stories
in the July 2008 collection:**

#13 THE ITALIAN
TYCOON'S MISTRESS
by CATHY WILLIAMS

#14 RUTHLESS BOSS, HIRED WIFE
by KATE HEWITT

#15 IN THE TYCOON'S BED
by KATHRYN ROSS

#16 THE RICH MAN'S
RELUCTANT MISTRESS
by MARGARET MAYO

REQUEST YOUR FREE BOOKS!

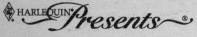 

2 FREE NOVELS PLUS 2 FREE GIFTS!

HP08

I ♥ HARLEQUIN *Presents*

BROUGHT TO YOU BY FANS OF HARLEQUIN PRESENTS.

We are its editors and authors and biggest fans—and we'd love to hear from YOU!

Subscribe today to our online blog at
www.iheartpresents.com